# "You bought her forgiveness, Nina."

"So what if I did?"

"Give her enough time and she'll come around without your having to resort to bribery."

"Time is the one thing I don't have on my side, don't you see? If I can't win her affection in the next six or seven weeks, I'm history."

"Affection that has to be bought isn't worth anything, Nina."

Right again, damn him! "Then what *does* make it worth something?"

Hugh inched closer. "This?" He brushed her eyelashes with his lips before moving his kiss down her cheek to find her mouth.

**CATHERINE SPENCER** suggests she turned to romance-fiction writing to keep from meddling in the love lives of her five daughters and two sons. The idea was that she would keep herself busy manipulating the characters in her novels instead. This, she says, has made everyone happy. In addition to writing novels, Catherine Spencer also plays the piano, collects antiques and grows tropical shrubs at her home in Vancouver, B.C., Canada.

Don't miss any of our special offers. Write to us at the following address for information on our newest releases.

Harlequin Reader Service
P.O. Box 1397, Buffalo, NY 14240
Canadian address: P.O. Box 603,
Fort Erie, Ont. L2A 5X3

# CATHERINE SPENCER

## Naturally Loving

## Harlequin Books

TORONTO • NEW YORK • LONDON
AMSTERDAM • PARIS • SYDNEY • HAMBURG
STOCKHOLM • ATHENS • TOKYO • MILAN
MADRID • WARSAW • BUDAPEST • AUCKLAND

For Sara,
who chose us and whom we've always
found so easy to love

Harlequin Presents first edition September 1993
ISBN 0-373-11587-3

Original hardcover edition published in 1992
by Mills & Boon Limited

NATURALLY LOVING

# CHAPTER ONE

NINA recognized them immediately. Not only were they the only people in the gazebo, but their attention was turned toward the parking area instead of the ocean view behind them. They were obviously waiting for something. Someone.

The man leaned against one of the archways, apparently relaxed, but even from a distance Nina sensed his tension. At her approach, he straightened and spoke to the girl, reaching out a hand to her and drawing her to her feet.

She's tall like her father, Nina thought.

*Or like me.*

The first genetic link! She hovered expectantly, waiting for some sign, something momentous. A clap of thunder, perhaps, or a chorus of celestial voices that only she could hear.

Nothing. Perhaps it was too soon. Perhaps she was still too far away for recognition to arc between them.

A gust of wind raced off the ocean and tugged playfully at her skirt, ballooning it into a parachute above her knees. Absently, she slapped it down, and wondered how the couple perceived her from their vantage point at the top of the steps that led up to the gazebo.

"How do I look?" she'd asked Sophie that morning, a lifetime ago it seemed now.

"Beautiful," the housekeeper had replied in heavily accented English. "What else?"

Nina had posed in front of the mirror, searching for something different, some sign. The same old face had stared back at her. "But do I look like a mother?" she'd persisted.

Sophie's shrug had spoken volumes, all of them wise. "Madame Nina, the question surely is do you *feel* like a mother?"

She hadn't then and she didn't now, despite the fact that she'd spent almost half her life striving toward this moment. She felt . . . not in control. She wasn't used to that and she didn't like it.

She had eight steps to climb before they could at last look each other in the eye. She knew because she counted each one, as though doing so would inspire her to say something when she reached the top that would break down the barriers she suddenly knew she'd have to overcome. On the seventh, she almost turned and ran.

The man spoke first. "Good morning," he said. "Are you . . . ?"

Nina nodded, and fixed her eyes on the girl. She saw a rather plain stranger. But the man—dear Lord!

"We guessed as much." He cleared his throat. "I'm Hugh Cavendish and this . . ." He cleared his throat again. "This is my daughter, Jane."

Unexpectedly, protest welled up in Nina. There'd been some bureaucratic mix-up. They'd found the wrong child.

But she's not *my* daughter! she wanted to cry.

Her daughter had been tiny and exquisite, with a sweet face and hair so dark and thick that all the nurses had exclaimed about it. This girl stood there awkward as a lump, anticipating rejection as though she expected people to be disappointed in her. Poor thing!

"I'm so glad to meet you," Nina said, and wondered if she should offer to shake hands or hug her.

"Hi," the girl replied, and slid out of reach behind her father.

He pulled her into the shelter of his arm and coaxed her forward again. "In difficult situations like this," he said, his smile too brief to do more than touch his mouth, "people can either eat or talk about the weather. We didn't have much of a breakfast and I don't think any of us really cares about the weather. Is there some place near where we could have lunch?"

Nina's stomach gave a tiny rumble of agreement. She hadn't eaten a proper meal in days, not since she'd first received word from the agency that the child she'd been coerced into placing for adoption at birth had registered to find her biological mother. "There's a place on the beach about half a mile away. They serve great seafood."

"Fish?" the girl inquired, her tone a condemnation.

"Shrimp, crab and oysters, mostly."

The girl made a face. "I think I'm allergic to that sort of stuff."

The father seemed surprised. "I didn't know that, Jane," he said.

She caught at the hair blowing in her eyes and shoved it ungracefully behind one ear. "It gives me zits," she said flatly. "Can't we go to McDonald's or something?"

Although she felt him glance questioningly her way, Nina fixed her attention on the girl. "Of course. There's one about five miles down the road. Shall we all go together?"

"We might as well follow behind," Hugh Cavendish said. "It'll save you having to drive us back out here later to pick up our car."

Nina hoped her relief didn't show. She'd been afraid he might accept her offer, or, worse yet, suggest the girl ride with her. She nodded. "In case we get separated, turn left at the second set of lights and you'll see the Arches over on the right."

They trooped down the steps, a trio separated by invisible chasms. No person in his right mind could possibly mistake them for a family. They were strangers so ill at ease that they couldn't wait to get away from one another.

Nina reached her car first and watched through the rear view mirror as he unlocked a dark blue Buick bearing Ontario license plates. The girl flung herself into the passenger seat and stared out of the side window, apparently ignoring her father, who placed a hand on her shoulder and spoke to her.

If she were mine, Nina thought, I'd teach her some manners.

She *is* yours.

It was enough to make her wish she could race away into the early lunch-hour traffic and lose the pair of them. This wasn't the way it was supposed to be. She had rehearsed this day for more than fifteen years, knew her entry, her cues, her lines, only to find now that she'd studied the wrong script. Something was missing: the tug of an unseen umbilical cord, or the sense of having at last caught up with her life.

They ate outside at a plastic table shaded by a plastic umbrella. "Would you like to come back to my house this afternoon and see where I live?" Nina asked, once they had their food set out in front of them.

"I'd rather take that gondola up Grouse Mountain," the girl said, cramming french fries into her mouth non-stop.

"That can wait, Jane," the father said. "We already agreed there'd be plenty of time later for sight-seeing."

"That's okay," Nina rushed to assure him. The room she'd optimistically prepared with white ruffled bedspread and sliding glass doors that opened out to the pool deck could wait, too—preferably for someone who'd appreciate it.

"Can I get a sundae, Dad?" The girl was half risen from the table before she'd finished asking.

"Perhaps," he chided her gently, "we'd all like one."

There was a moment's tense silence before she addressed Nina, staring all the while at the dome of the umbrella. "You want me to get you something?"

"Coffee would be nice," Nina said, surreptitiously checking her bag to make sure her pager was turned on. Surely somebody out there in the normal world needed her services about now.

"I realize this isn't easy," the father observed, once they were alone, "but it doesn't help to have you fidgeting for an excuse to get away from her."

Shocked by his perception, Nina dared to look at him again. His dark hair was prematurely frosted with gray and he had extraordinarily light blue eyes made all the more arresting by a tan too deep to have been acquired in Ontario. He was studying her, too, but she felt as though he saw past her features to her soul. Unnerved, she averted her face. "Why did she register with the agency? She doesn't seem to want to know me," she said, struggling to collect her thoughts.

He shrugged in faint apology. "It wasn't exactly her idea. I'm the one who encouraged her to come looking for you."

"Why?"

"She's a very unhappy child. You know her mother died three years ago, and there hasn't been anyone else to take her place. Jane's going on sixteen and she needs a woman's touch." Again that smile, a little warmer this time. "Who better than you?"

"Is there no one closer?"

He raised reproving brows. "Closer than you, her birth mother, Miss Sommers?"

Nina shied away from the prospect of so much responsibility. It had seemed easy to make all the right responses when they'd communicated long distance by telephone and carefully worded letters. Even the slightly out-of-focus snapshots they'd exchanged had preserved a sense of false confidence. Actual confrontation was much less forgiving, allowing for no such self-indulgence. "Other family, perhaps?" she ventured. "People she's known for years?"

He examined his hands, which gave her the opportunity to study him again. He was a big man but too thin, with a look of convalescence about him that no amount of healthy tan could quite disguise. He had a strong face, pared lean to display proud cheekbones and a stubborn jaw. Laughter had etched lines beside his eyes, and, for all that he looked so stern now, the natural curve of his mouth suggested a capacity for tenderness that she thought might be impossible to resist.

"None who matters," he finally admitted.

It was Nina's turn to be surprised. "Friends, then?"

He glanced up, capturing her expression. "If you didn't want the job of mothering her," he asked, his light blue eyes chilly with disapproval, "why did you so actively pursue the search for her?"

"Because, although I placed her for adoption when she was only a week old, not a day has gone by since when I haven't thought about her, and wondered if she was happy and loved and well cared for." She raised her shoulders eloquently. "I had to find out."

He made no effort to mitigate the censure in his voice. "Yet you did choose to give her up."

The temptation to account for those long-ago decisions tugged at her, but she thrust it aside. She supposed, if she owed anyone explanations, it was this man and his daughter, but she would not let either of them bully her into defensive revelations of her most private and painful secrets. She already knew that, to some people, there was no justification for what she had done. He would have to show himself less ready to condemn before she shared with him the exact circumstances that had led to her being pregnant at sixteen. Until he did, she would not be provoked into discussing them.

"Yes, I chose to give her up, Mr. Cavendish, but that doesn't explain why she is so alone now."

"She spent a lot of time away at different schools since her mother died," he explained, then hesitated as though debating how much he dared confide in her. "She was asked to leave the last two."

Pity stabbed her, for the daughter, of course, but more for him. He seemed very alone and almost as unsure of his proper role as Nina was of hers. She had often wondered what sort of people had taken her baby for their own, but the real focus of her hopes and prayers had always been her child. It had never occurred to her, when she heard he was bringing the girl to meet her, that her attention would be drawn more toward the father, that he would be the one to tap deep wells of emotion within her.

Nina folded her hands to prevent herself from reaching across and touching him in sympathy. "Do you want to tell me why?"

"Not here." He inclined his head towards where the girl was coming back to join them. "But I do think we should talk some time soon. No matter how difficult it might be, we need to try to understand and support each other, if this is to work out for her."

Nina felt in her purse for a business card and handed it to him. "You already know where I live, but if it's less awkward I can also be reached through my office. A message will be forwarded to me if I happen to be in court that day."

The girl plunked down the coffee so hard that it splashed dangerously close to the cuff of Nina's shantung jacket. "Here," she muttered. "I didn't know what you wanted in it so I brought sugar and cream."

Almost goaded into letting her annoyance show, Nina lifted her gaze to the girl's, expecting to meet truculence. Instead, she caught a flash of apprehension quickly masked behind defiance: You don't like me and I don't care, it said.

For the first time since they'd met, Nina felt a glimmer of something brighter than despair. Contrary to what her expression tried to convey, the girl cared.

"She doesn't look like my mother." Jane nibbled furiously on the cuticle of her left thumb. "Do you think she does, Daddy?"

"I'm not sure."

"Do you think she's pretty?"

He thought she was the most beautiful creature he'd ever come across, but now did not seem the politic time to say so. Instead he sought refuge in semantics. "Hmm...no, I don't think I'd call her pretty."

Jane sighed and reviewed her mangled cuticle with satisfaction. "Good. Where are we going now?"

"Back to the house to finish unpacking, then I thought we'd go out and find a place to eat dinner. Maybe visit Chinatown. Would you like that?"

"Sure. Did you notice her shoes? Why do you suppose she wears such high heels? It's as if she wants everybody to notice how tall she is."

He laughed. "Not everyone thinks being tall is an affliction, Janie."

She slouched low in the seat. "I hate it. I wish I was little, like Mother."

He let that pass. There was no use trying to force-feed the obvious. "You weren't very friendly toward her, you know."

"So? She wasn't very nice to me, either. You saw the way she looked at me. She thought I was totally gross."

"Perhaps," he said, trying to be fair, "she was nervous of doing or saying the wrong thing."

"What's she got to be nervous about? I'm the one on trial."

He drew up outside the gateway to the town house complex, braking sharply, and swung around to face her. "Why would you say something like that? No one's on trial here."

"You want her to check me out," she muttered sullenly, "for when you go away again."

For all that it wasn't the truth, she'd come close enough to recognizing his motives to make him uncomfortable. "I want you to give her a chance to get to know you, Janie, because I know that if you do she'll like you, and I happen to think we can never have too many friends.''

She was a bright girl, not easily sidetracked. "*Are* you going away again?''

''Not if I can help it and certainly not in the next couple of months. We've planned to spend the summer together out here and nothing's going to change that.''

Too often, she held herself aloof from him, her expression so closed that he didn't know whether she was pleased by his reappearance in her life or not. Sometimes, when he looked for the little girl he used to know, he could hardly find her in the emerging woman. Now, however, she suddenly switched back to childhood, flinging herself at him and winding long, skinny arms around his neck to hug him tightly. "Nothing? Not even her?''

He couldn't help himself. It was his job now, after all. "She,'' he said.

Jane giggled impishly. "*She*'s the cat's mother!''

More like the cat's miaow, he thought, and assumed a suitably severe expression. "Watch your manners, miss.''

''Did you notice,'' Jane said, pulling back to her own side of the car, "that she didn't bother asking us again if we wanted to go to her place?''

''Why would she, considering the response she got from you the first time? You gave the impression you couldn't care less.''

''But *she*'s supposed to care! She's supposed to feel guilty and want to make up for what she did.''

''For God's sake, Jane, who filled your head with that sort of nonsense?'' As if he needed to ask! It was the sort of remark that had Sandra's name stamped all over it.

* * *

"One look at your face and I think it's as well that to-morrow is Sunday," Sophie announced, as Nina came up the path from the garage and let herself in through the kitchen door. "Dare I ask how it went?"

"Whatever it was I expected," Nina said, slumping onto a stool at the breakfast bar, "I didn't get it. Don't ask me how, but we got off on the wrong foot and there was no setting things right."

"Give it time, *ma chère*." Sophie hulled strawberries, selected one that she considered perfection, and popped it into Nina's mouth with all the comfortable familiarity that came from knowing that her friendship was valued as much as her domestic services. "When she tastes my good French-Canadian cooking, she will relent."

Nina helped herself to another berry, and contemplated it gloomily. "I don't think so. I invited them both here and she turned me down flat."

"So ask again. Tell her the swimming pool is too big for one person."

"Bribe her?" Nina was scandalized. The experts who wrote those books on how to bring up children would never approve.

Sophie rolled her eyes. "*Mon Dieu*, we are not in court now! When my little ones did not like the taste of what was good for them, I covered it in catsup. Soon, they forgot what was underneath and cleaned their plates, and I..." She smiled hugely. "I won the war without a battle."

Did it really all boil down to something that simple? Remembering the hostility and awkwardness of the morning, Nina doubted it. But then again, there had been that moment at the end, with the coffee, when she'd looked at the girl and seen herself at the same age. Adolescence, as she remembered only too well, had been totally unbearable. "Maybe it's worth a try," she agreed. "What do I have to lose?"

"Nothing," the housekeeper told her cheerfully. "Your heart has been empty like your arms for nearly sixteen years. Now, tell me about the meeting. *La petite—* how did she look?"

Nina shrugged helplessly. "Ordinary."

"Then give thanks," Sophie laughed. "She does not have diaper pins in her nose, and she has not painted her hair blue."

"No. She has light brown hair with bangs that need trimming, and her eyes..." Nina's answering smile faded. "I'm not sure. They might be hazel."

But the father's were the color of rare blue topaz, his silvering hair thick and well barbered.

"She is a happy child?"

"Apparently not."

Sophie clucked sympathy. "And the papa, what about him?"

He terrified her. She'd hardly dared look at him because all the things she'd expected to find in the child— that electricity, that sense of her destiny having at last found its nesting place—she'd discovered instead in the father. Ask me to describe the kind of man I've looked for all my life, she felt like saying, and I'll describe Hugh Cavendish. "He seems a nice enough man."

"Madame Nina," Sophie said softly, "if this is so, why does he trouble you so much?"

Nina attempted a laugh. "He doesn't trouble me, Sophie. If anything, he's an ally."

"You believe this?"

"Of course. We're on the same side."

Sophie reached for the handset of the phone. "Then there is no reason to delay," she declared, handing it to

Nina. "Call and tell him there is room enough for *two* more in the pool."

"Next week, perhaps. I'll give them a chance to settle in first."

"Why, when you have only a few weeks in which to make up for so many lost years, would you waste even one day?"

The handset inched closer, the perforations in its mouthpiece like eyes lined up and watching her. There was no ignoring it. "They probably aren't even home," Nina hedged. "She wanted to go sight-seeing."

"Such waste," Sophie intoned, extending the aerial and waving it like a conductor's baton to lend emphasis to her words. "And such fear."

Resigned, Nina took the phone and punched in the number he'd given her. She'd let it ring six times. If no one answered by then, she, at least, would be off the hook.

# CHAPTER TWO

HUGH CAVENDISH answered on the second ring. Undistracted by his appearance this time, Nina found her imagination captured instead by the baritone sound of him. The richness of his voice conveyed impressions of strength teamed with stability, of power tempered by integrity. No wonder she was so drawn to him. He was the antithesis of all the other men who'd ever been a part of her life.

"I know we didn't plan this, and I'll understand if you'd prefer not to accept until we've had a chance to talk," she said, thrusting aside her fanciful notions, "but I thought you and—er—your daughter might like to spend some time here over the weekend. It's supposed to be hot again, and I have a pool."

The silence that followed bore home to her how incredibly crass she'd managed to make the invitation sound. Let me show off my toys, she might as well have said. They'll change your child's opinion of me. "What I mean——" she began, but he cut her off.

"What you mean is that we can lead the horse to water and hope she'll decide to drink," he replied, and she could tell from the way his voice sounded, with a sort of lilt to it, that he was smiling.

"If it's that obvious, we should probably forget it."

"No!" he said sharply. "Let me accept for both of us, before you rescind the invitation. Which day, what time?"

18

She tried to subdue her pleasure. "Tomorrow, at three? That leaves you plenty of time to do other things in the morning."

"We'll look forward to it."

They were half an hour late arriving, time enough for Nina to grow despairing at the realization of how much she wanted to see them both again. When she heard the car pull up outside the front door, which faced northeast toward the distant mountains, she had to stop herself from racing out to greet them. After yesterday's cool reception, she knew enough not to count on any great show of enthusiasm from the daughter, and had no business expecting anything at all from the man.

He was bent over the trunk, unloading their bags, a small canvas tote for him and a carry-all for her that would have had to fly cargo in a passenger jet. "What *didn't* you bring, Janie?" Nina heard him ask with dry humor.

"It's just my stuff, ' the girl said, then noticing Nina at the open front door, muttered, "Hey, Dad, she's here."

He straightened up, slamming the trunk lid closed as he did so. "Hi! Sorry we're late. Your directions were great, but my navigator doesn't know her left from her right. We almost ended up crossing the border into the States."

"No problem," Nina told him, thinking it was about as inappropriate a reply as she could have come up with, considering the girl was eyeing her with all the dedicated curiosity of a scientist confronting a new and dangerous form of life.

"Say hello, Jane," her father prompted her.

"Hi." The eyes, more green than hazel, discovered Nina's painted toenails and refused to budge.

"Come in and I'll show you where you can change," Nina said, compensating for her own lack of greeting by touching the girl lightly on the back. She was even thinner than her father, her shoulder blades protruding like budding wings on either side of her spine. When she felt Nina's hand on her, she shied away, as appalled as if the evil witch from *Hansel and Gretel* were testing her for oven readiness.

Hugh Cavendish noticed and rushed to fill the awkward pause. "Sounds good to me," he said. "I think we're both ready for a swim. It's even hotter out here than it is downtown."

"Much drier, too. We get only about a third of the rain that falls in the city," Nina said, and hurried them through the house, hoping they wouldn't notice that Sophie had one eager eye pressed up against the kitchen door which stood open a crack. This was not the time for introductions, nor was she up to fielding her house-keeper's astute observations. The vibes, as some of her youthful clients were fond of saying, were already not good. "I'll wait for you outside by the pool. You can change in the cabana below the terrace."

He joined her first, a pair of sunglasses in his hand and a towel slung around his neck. "Jane's still changing and probably will be for the next hour," he said. "How can she take so long to get ready?"

Nina smiled. "It'll get worse as she grows older."

"Spare me!" he groaned, then cocked his head to one side, his expression inscrutable. "Well, are you ready for round two?"

She shrugged. "It can only get better, surely?"

"I hope so." Dropping his towel and glasses on a chaise, he looked around, taking in the tubs of flowering plants on the terrace adjoining the pool deck, and the little waterfall that splashed over a fern-clad slab of granite into the pool itself. "Very tasteful," he commented, but there was reluctance in his tone, as though he disapproved of what he saw.

"Thank you," she murmured, and popped her own sunglasses on her nose so that she could inspect him unobserved. His tailored swimming trunks revealed a wonderful body, even though it was a bit underweight. None of that loose skin or softness she might have expected. If it weren't for his hair, he could pass for a man in his late twenties, but she knew he had to be older, forty at the very least, to have adopted Jane nearly sixteen years ago.

She also knew her glasses didn't disguise the fact that she was staring, nor that the silence spinning out between the two of them had lasted too long. She gestured toward the pool. "Don't feel you have to be polite."

"I won't, thanks. It looks too good to waste."

He swam well, with the sort of easy rhythm that some people seemed to be born with. Wet, his hair shone dark, the gray hidden. Added to his natural coordination and the definition of muscle beneath the deeply tanned skin, it underlined a youthful vitality, yet he had the face of a man who'd known suffering.

A movement on the upper deck caught her attention. The girl stood stiffly in the lee of the terrace, silently watching Nina watch him.

Nina waved. "Come on down and enjoy," she called. "It's too hot to sit up there."

She inched down the steps, lugging her bag with her, the picture of uneasiness in her plain black swimsuit.

She had fair skin, the kind that would burn easily, and was all bones and sharp angles.

"Go join your father," Nina invited, and decided that if the day ever came that the girl cast her in a more sympathetic role she'd take her shopping. It was bad enough having to be fifteen and ungainly, without having to wear something that looked as if it were part of the uniform from a reform school.

"I don't feel like it right now. I'd rather read." She spread out her towel at a safe distance and rummaged around in her bag, unearthing a bottle of sun cream, a hairbrush, elastics and barrettes, and a copy of the latest teenage gothic thriller.

Noticing her arrival, her father swam over and hauled himself out to join her. "You okay, Janie?"

Nina couldn't hear the reply, probably because she wasn't intended to. A few minutes later, Jane got up and went to sit on the edge of the pool. He left her dangling her legs in the water and, toweling himself off, came back to Nina.

"How's she doing?" she asked, nodding toward Jane.

He settled on a chaise in the shade of a magnolia tree and combed his fingers through his hair. "She feels awkward, out of place."

"I gathered as much." Nina poured white grape juice over freshly crushed mint in tall stemmed glasses, and handed one to him. "Was it hard convincing her to spend the afternoon here?"

"That's the crazy part. She was quite eager when she heard you'd invited us. Now that she's here, though . . ." He shook his head and held up his glass, apparently absorbed in the prisms of light trapped in its contents, and caught her off guard with his sudden change of topic. "How come," he asked, "you never call her Jane?"

"What do you mean?" Flustered, Nina refolded a tiny linen napkin and placed it on the table beside him.

He swung his gaze to her, plying her with a look from those steely blue eyes that saw past all the subterfuge. "You know what I mean. Outwardly, you refer to her as 'you' or 'her' or 'my daughter.'" Amusement flickered over his mouth. "And heaven only knows what you call her when no one's around to hear."

Nina had the grace to blush. "Does it make me sound terribly immature if I say that she doesn't call me anything, either?"

He laughed, perfect teeth flashing against his dark features. "Then I guess she's more your daughter than either of us realizes!"

Some of Nina's tension dissipated at that. "Anyone would think," she admitted ruefully, "that I'm not used to teenagers, the way I'm behaving."

"You see much of them in your job?"

She nodded. "I work in conjunction with the juvenile offenders' office. I'm a sort of public defender for minors who can't afford legal representation."

"I thought that was what probation officers were for. I didn't realize juveniles needed legal representation as well."

"Often they don't, but if they're involved with older kids who fall under the jurisdiction of adult court they can get caught between two systems and need someone to intercede for them. Then there are those who are return offenders. Someone has to go to bat for them, too."

He frowned. "Why? Maybe they should learn to respect the law the hard way."

"For kids who've never had the chance to crawl out from under the poverty and indifference they were born into, there's only one law that applies: survival at any cost. And to answer your question, I take the time to care because too often there isn't anyone else who does. No child should have to grow up knowing that."

"No," he agreed, an oddly bleak expression crossing his face, "no child should." He looked over at her again, acknowledging the curiosity his remark had aroused in her. "We know so little about each other. Why does it seem as if there shouldn't be any secrets between us?"

Did he feel it, too, then, that sense of having found a part of himself in a stranger? "Silly, isn't it?" she conceded. "When all we have in common is...Jane." The name fumbled awkwardly past her lips.

"Now that you've met her," he asked, "do you have any regrets?"

She didn't know how to answer him. Of course she had regrets. She'd hoped for so much, felt so cheated. But would continued ignorance have been easier to bear? She wasn't sure. "I think it's too soon to decide."

She heard him sigh. "Thank you for that," he said and touched her hand briefly. "To get back to what we were talking about before we got sidetracked, I think Jane doesn't call you anything because she doesn't know what you expect. You're her natural mother but she obviously wouldn't be comfortable saying 'Mom,' and 'Miss Sommers' goes too far the other way. So, like you, she plays it safe and sticks to 'her' and 'she.'"

Jane was in the water, swimming cautious lengths as though she hoped no one would notice that she might be having a good time. "She should call me Nina."

"Why don't you tell her so?"

And get the brush-off? Nina felt like retorting, but he favored her with that charming smile which made the risk seem worthwhile. Slipping free of her cover-up, she rose and walked toward the pool, feeling his eyes following her and her emerald green swimsuit with its low-cut back.

What did he see? A well-heeled yuppie, bored enough to think she wanted to find her lost daughter? A successful lawyer, lonely for the other children she might have had if only she hadn't devoted herself to a career? Or a woman with olive-toned skin and long legs whom he'd like to get to know better for reasons unconnected with anyone else?

Diving shallowly, she surfaced beside the girl and kept pace with her until they reached the far end of the pool. "Hey, you look pretty good in the water."

Jane's eyes were pink from the chlorine and she blinked angrily as though trying to rid herself of it and all the other irritations to which she was presently subjected. "Oh, right! Like better than on land near you, you mean."

"I beg your pardon?"

"I saw the way you were looking at my father."

Debating the wisdom of ignoring the remark, Nina decided that, at the present rate of progress, summer would be well on its way to winter before she made a dent in the girl's hostility. One thing she'd learned in her work was to trust her instincts. Right now, they were urging her to take a stand or else prepare to engage in verbal skirmishes for the next two months or more. "And how was that?" she inquired.

"Like you wished I wasn't here."

"Maybe if you made more of an effort to be pleasant that would change."

Jane's mouth dropped open in shock. "Oh, fine thing!" she muttered, treading water and glaring. "Why'd you go to all the trouble of finding me if you feel like that?"

It seemed best to keep things simple. "I was curious."

"I bet."

"I wanted to know about you, what you looked like, what you liked doing, what sort of life you had."

"Now you know, I suppose you wish you hadn't bothered."

"I don't wish any such thing."

Jane snorted in disgust and dunked herself, emerging like a seal with her face turned up to the sun and her bangs plastered back wetly against her skull. "You're such a liar!"

"And you're very rude."

"You're not my mother."

Hanging on to the side of the pool and idly stroking with her legs, Nina prayed for wisdom. And forbearance. "I'd like to be your friend."

Jane flung a disbelieving glance heavenward. "People your age don't want to be friends with kids my age."

"You're right, they don't. How about if I say instead that I'd like to get to know you?"

"Why? I don't even look like you."

"No, you're fair, like——"

"Like my mother was. Everyone says I look exactly like her, except..." She stopped and ventured a suspicious glance at Nina. "Were you tall when you were my age?"

Here it came when she was least expecting it, the first tentative reaching out that she'd been hoping for. A tiny glow warmed Nina's heart. "Like a beanpole," she confessed. "I hated going to school dances because I was taller than most of the guys in my class."

"I should have known it was all your fault." Jane glowered, severing the fragile bond without mercy.

"Most of them caught up and passed me eventually," Nina offered lamely. As a placation, it left a lot to be desired, but it was the best she could come up with on such short notice. "And fashion designers love tall women."

Jane hauled sullenly on her swimsuit straps, which repeatedly slipped from her shoulders, and delivered her parting shot. "Maybe when the women are as old as you," she said, then performed a neat backward somersault and raced back to the shallow end of the pool, beating Nina by a nose.

Knowing she'd won that round seemed to improve Jane's disposition. As quickly as it had arisen, her antagonism vanished and she turned suddenly chatty. Picking up a towel, she mopped water from her face and hair, then flung herself down on one of the chaises.

"Do you live here by yourself?" she asked, taking stock of her surroundings.

"Except for Sophie, yes. Would you like some juice?"

Jane eyed the glass her father held. "Some of that, you mean?"

"Yes."

She grew pink with excitement. "I guess so. What's the green stuff?"

"Mint."

"That's what I thought." She leaned back, crossing her legs with feigned nonchalance. "Who's Sophie?"

"Mrs. Légère, my housekeeper," Nina replied, noticing that Hugh's feet seemed to be affording him a wealth of quiet diversion. "Shall I put your drink down here?" She indicated a small side table.

"Oh, sure." Jane eyed the glass again, pure delight mixed with apprehension in her gaze. "What sort of juice is it?'' she asked, as though she suspected it might be hemlock.

"Grape. If you'd prefer it sparkling, I can add a squirt of soda water.''

"That's okay." Nervously, she picked up the glass by the stem and, trying to hold it steady and extend her pinkie at the same time, sipped experimentally.

Nina's heart turned over. For one tiny second, she thought she glimpsed a ghost from her past in the wide-eyed uncertainty she detected on the girl's face. How young she suddenly looked, and how defenseless.

Then the moment passed. Confidence restored, Jane sat up straighter, apparently having reached a decision. "I like it here," she allowed graciously. "It's a lot better than the place we're staying in."

As a compliment, it was entirely too oblique for Nina to be able to lay personal claim to it, but she never-theless grabbed at the opportunity it presented. "You're welcome to stay here if you'd like to," she offered. "There's room."

Jane chewed on her fingernail meditatively. "For my father, too?"

"Of course," Nina replied, squashing a little uprising of panic. He could have the suite above the garage, which was quite self-contained and far enough removed from her bedroom for her to keep her fantasies under control.

"Jane," Hugh said, a trace of annoyance displacing his former amusement, "the house we're renting is charming and more than adequate for two people."

"It doesn't have a pool."

"You'll survive. Half the people in the world don't have decent drinking water, let alone the luxury of a pool."

"So what?" The sullenness was back in full force. "Making me miserable isn't going to stop them from being thirsty."

"Jane . . . !"

Nina exchanged a glance with him. "It's up to you, of course, but I'd really like to have you here."

Intercepting the look, Jane switched tactics and rushed to support the idea. "It would give me a chance to get to know her, Daddy. Isn't that what you said you wanted?"

The little minx, Nina thought, watching with interest to see how Hugh handled such brazen manipulation.

With a marked lack of tolerance, she soon discovered.

"We'll talk about it later, Jane. And our hostess's name is Nina."

"But I thought the whole point——"

"That's enough," he warned her curtly, the humorous curve of his lips flattening into a thin line. "Go get changed and pack up your stuff. We might as well leave now if you're going to spoil the rest of the afternoon by arguing."

"That's what you always do!" the girl stormed, flinging herself out of the chair so suddenly that her juice spilled over. "You always just change the subject when you can't give me a good reason for not doing something. I don't know why we even bothered to come all the way out here if we're going to spend most of our time crammed in that house in the middle of downtown. I wish you'd left me at home."

"The way you're behaving right now," he said with deadly sincerity, "I wish I had, too."

Jane's eyes filled with sudden tears. Averting her face, she collected her possessions and disappeared inside the house, slapping her sandals noisily up the steps and over the terrace to camouflage her distress.

"You know," Nina offered, once she and Hugh were alone again, "she does have a point—about our getting to know one another, I mean."

"Let's get something straight from the outset," he said shortly, staring after Jane with obvious exasperation. "I'm not about to let the pair of you gang up on me whenever it happens to suit you. I'm the one who makes the decisions, not you. You gave up that right a long time ago."

He must have heard her gasp of dismay, because he immediately closed his eyes and punched a coiled fist lightly against forehead. "Forget I said that, please!"

"I'm not trying to interfere," Nina protested. "It's just that I thought we were on the verge of establishing some sort of rapport, and——"

"And I sabotaged it by asserting my authority." He sighed heavily. "Look, Miss Sommers—Nina—I'm pretty new at this parenting business myself, but I don't need the latest text on raising a teenager to tell me that confrontations like the one you just witnessed are best avoided. It's sometimes damned hard, though, to draw the line between being fair and being permissive."

"Then let me help you where I can."

He drained his glass and stood up. "You don't know what you'd be letting yourself in for," he said wryly.

"I'd manage." Nina inclined her head consideringly. "Forgive me for saying so, but I think you could use some help. You seem . . ." She shrugged, at a loss to pinpoint exactly what it was about him that troubled her. "I don't know . . . depleted, somehow."

"I've been running on adrenalin too long, that's all." He shook his head. "I don't know, perhaps it was a mistake to bring Jane here before you and I had a chance to talk privately. All I do know is that I feel hopelessly inadequate when it comes to dealing with my daughter and I hate it. I'm used to being in charge and having everything under control."

She could have told him that nothing was ever under complete control where teenagers were concerned, but she knew he'd resent the advice. Instead, she touched his arm sympathetically. "Then let's arrange to meet some time soon and see if we can't come up with a mutual support system. And in case you're wondering, I wasn't being noble with the invitation to stay here. It stands, for as long as you're in the area."

He shook her off almost angrily. "No," he said.

She withdrew her hand as though he'd slapped at it. "Whatever you think is best, of course. When may I see Jane again?"

He laughed shortly. "I'm surprised you want to."

"So am I," she admitted. "but just when I'm about ready to throw up my hands and walk away from the whole situation she does something that brings my own miserable adolescence back to me so vividly that all I want to do is wrap my arms around her and hug all the anger out of her."

"I profoundly hope you won't give in to that urge," he said with droll horror, "at least not until things improve. Knowing Jane as I do, I suspect the outcome could be disastrous."

It hadn't been an afternoon memorable for its light-heartedness, yet she found herself laughing with him. "We really do need to get together and map out our campaign strategy, don't we?"

"The sooner, the better." He smiled at her almost conspiratorially. "How's your schedule next week?"

They were isolated in the hush of early evening. The sun had dipped behind the island hills and left the western sky a luminous apricot. The rest of the world might have been a million miles distant. The way he was looking at her, the near smile on his mouth and the sudden keen observation in those remarkable eyes, caused a slow heat to run through her.

"Not bad," she said, picking up the cotton shift she'd discarded earlier. "Court schedules are pretty light during the summer."

Jane was waiting in the car, huddled against the passenger door to put as much distance as possible between her and the driver's seat.

"Well, there's no doubt I'm in the dog house," Hugh muttered under his breath, shooting an amused glance at Nina.

She felt her mouth twitch dangerously and made an effort to control it. Now was not a good time for them to appear to be sharing a private joke at Jane's expense. "I'm so glad you stopped by, both of you."

Although she must have heard, Jane kept her face stubbornly turned away.

"And I thank you—for both of us." Hugh's raised shoulders bespoke apology. "I'll be in touch."

Please make it soon, Nina almost said, and stopped herself just in time. What was it about him that made her want to ignore the circumstances under which they'd met, and simply follow primal instinct? She was too worldly, too sophisticated, to be swayed by a pair of steel blue eyes, or a smile that could melt an ice cap. Only the very innocent or the very foolish allowed the seeds of passion to take root in such shallow soil.

He was watching her. Quietly. Knowingly.

"Goodbye," she said, and stepped inside the house before she embarrassed both of them.

He thought, as he drove back to the city, that it might as well have been Sandra beside him. Same hunched, narrow shoulders, same wall of hostility that had always seemed to rise up between them on the way home from social events. It had been almost eleven years since the divorce, with Jane not yet in school, but it all came back now, reminding him of one of the first lessons he'd learned: there was no understanding women.

"What's the matter?" he must have inquired a thousand times in the early years of the marriage, never sure how he'd managed to provoke Sandra's resentment. He didn't drink too much, he didn't tell obscene jokes, and he didn't chase other women.

"If you have to ask, what's the point in talking about it?" she'd invariably reply, her profile remote.

And he'd cast about in his mind for things he might have done. Or not done. And in the course of the next day or so, she'd let him know, dropping meager little clues with words, and following them with long, accusatory silences. He'd honed his powers of deduction to formidable heights on those silences.

"Jane," he said now, not taking his eyes off the road ahead, "I didn't like that scene back at Nina's, but I like what's going on now even less. We both know why I got annoyed, and I'm sorry if I embarrassed you by letting it show. Now tell me why you're so angry, and let's deal with it."

"What's the point? You won't listen."

Rage caught him by surprise. He slammed his palm down flat on the dash. "Damn it, Jane, I am listening, so talk to me!"

His anger almost had her jumping out of her seat. She shrank from him.

"Please," he said, lowering his voice.

"I don't know how I'm supposed to feel," she said, her words trembling on the edge of tears. "You want me to get along with her. You said I had to do my part and cooperate—give her a chance, you said, because it's hard for her, too. Well, this afternoon, I tried, and you treated me like a dumb baby."

"Taking advantage of someone for the things she owns that she's willing to share with you isn't cooperating, Jane," he said carefully, hating what he thought he heard in her voice, the same materialistic avarice that had driven Sandra. "That's using her. It's the person she is that matters, not what she's got."

"I'm trying to like her, Daddy, but it's hard."

"Why? What is it that you find so hard?"

He saw that she'd shredded the tissue she'd fished out of her bag, that she was worrying a hangnail on her finger until it bled. He thought she was going to refuse to answer and he had his mouth half open, ready to insist, when she finally spoke.

"I wonder how Mother would feel, if she knew. It's as if I'm betraying her. Like today when we were in the pool, *she* started talking and I wanted to ask questions. I was interested, you know? Then I remembered what Mother always said about the kind of women who give their babies away——"

"Jane, we discussed that when I first mentioned trying to find Nina. I thought I'd made you understand."

"But Mother wouldn't understand, Daddy! She'd think I was turning my back on her. I feel stuck in the middle. You want me to think one way, and Mother wants me to think another."

Even from the grave, Sandra, you're pulling your little stunts. He felt a muscle twitch in his jaw. "You can't possibly know that, honey, because if your mother were still alive this situation would never have arisen."

She lifted her shoulders, whether in disbelief or agreement he couldn't tell. "Even so," she said.

"Even so what? Don't shut me out, Janie. I'm not very good at reading your mind."

"Even if you're right, how well are we going to get to know her if we just see her once every few days? It took us a week to drive out here, and it'll take that long to go back home. That leaves us about eight weeks. It just seems to make more sense, if she wants it, for us to stay at her place, that's all. But the way you jumped all over me this afternoon, it's as if you're afraid we might like her too much, instead of not enough."

Out of the mouths of babes! he thought, pulling up outside the smart town-house complex. The lights from Granville Island made the shadows seem darker and brought dusk closer. Music, carried across the water by the breeze, drifted through the open windows of the car. To the north, mountain peaks spread darkly across the pale sky, an impressive setting for the jewel of the city sprawled at their feet. Suddenly, he was tired of fighting.

"Go change into something pretty and brush your hair, and we'll have dinner at one of the waterfront restaurants on the Island," he said, when they were inside the front door of the house.

He was just putting her off, he knew. What she'd said about Nina made more sense than he cared to admit, but he wasn't up to dealing with it right now. It could wait another day.

The beginnings of a headache threatened, stabbing distantly behind his left eye. Annoyed, he went into the bathroom off the master bedroom and filled a glass with water, deciding he was going soft in his old age if he couldn't handle minor stress without falling apart. He was in friendly territory, for Pete's sake, not a prison cell in Colombia. And he was dealing with his daughter, instead of a bunch of hostile rebels whose attitudes were as primitive as the jungle they inhabited. Hardly a reason to haul out the painkillers.

Except he knew there was more to it than that. "I wasn't being noble with the invitation to stay here," Nina had said, laying her cool, elegant fingertips on his arm. "It stands."

But he'd been noble when he'd shaken her off, and again when he'd tried to look away as she pulled on the thing she'd worn on top of her swimsuit. She'd slipped it over her head and shaken her long, dark hair into place with the same innate grace she exhibited in all her movements, and, unable to help himself, he'd studied her as if she were the first woman he'd ever seen. She had dramatically beautiful eyes, dark and powerfully seductive, just like the rest of her. She tugged at every erotic nerve he possessed. Living in proximity with her, especially given the circumstances, was unthinkable. Surely she understood that?

Then again, perhaps she didn't. Perhaps he'd lived in site camps for so many years that he'd forgotten how to behave in the company of a beautiful, sophisticated woman. She was merely being polite and he—oh, he'd be a damn fool to think, even for a moment, that she was different from other women. They were all the same: complicated creatures whose powers of reasoning were so closely linked to hormones and instinct that they seldom relied on logic. He'd left it at least ten years too late to be persuaded otherwise, and, even if the timing had been right, she was all wrong. He only had to look at her house to realize that.

"Get it together, Cavendish," he told his reflection in the beveled mirror of the medicine cabinet, "and stop being such a glutton for punishment. You don't need any more complications in your life, especially not now."

Jane's scream floated down the stairs just as he swallowed the analgesic, and he heard her call his name over and over, her voice shrill with terror.

lace been right, the useful wrong subterfuge had to stop before it began to cost too dear.

Tired to begging, Georgianna, in another characteristic-
ally brusque volley of the marriage suit met... And she stopped abruptly, blinking away the tears. She'd only need... more contrandictions in acute pity, especially not to

## CHAPTER THREE

HILARY, her secretary, was answering the phone when Nina stepped from the elevator into the reception area shortly after three on Monday afternoon. "For you," she said quietly, covering the mouthpiece with her free hand. "A Hugh Cavendish. It's the fourth time he's called."

"Put him through." Elation had her pulse racing in top gear. *Next week*, he'd said, which could have meant any time from Monday to Saturday, but ever since she woke up that morning she'd been hoping that he'd phone today. When she picked up the receiver in her office and heard his voice, however, her mouth ran suddenly dry and an unpleasantly erratic thudding inside her chest displaced her pleasure.

Something was terribly wrong.

"I need to see you as soon as possible," he began, jumping right in without so much as a "Hi, how are you?" "When would be a good time?"

Nina knew controlled alarm when she heard it. It slithered over the line, pervasive as fog, touching her all over with clammy dread. "Hugh, has something happened?"

"What about this evening, right after work? Can you make it then?"

"Yes," she said. "Where do you want to meet?"

"Somewhere close to the place I'm renting in False Creek. I don't want to be too far away, just in case..."

"I understand," she said, not understanding at all. Whatever the reason for his anxiety to see her, it clearly had nothing to do with the anticipated pleasure of her company. She flipped through the card index she kept on her desk which listed her favorite restaurants. "There's a little Guatemalan place at the bottom of Bootleg Alley. It's right on the water and only about five minutes' walk from where you are. I've got one more appointment that I have to take care of, but I can meet you about five-thirty. Is that soon enough?"

"It'll have to be," he replied, and hung up.

She arrived nearly ten minutes early but even then he'd beaten her to it. She found him at a white wicker table in a corner of the courtyard. A pergola, heavy with flowering vines, kept the carafe of wine set in front of him out of the sun and sent shadows flitting over his features. With his dark tan, he could have passed for the ex-patriot lord of some tropical island, come to enjoy the ambience of this little oasis of hospitality so reminiscent of home. Until one looked in his eyes and saw the bleakness there, or noticed the white-knuckled tension of his fingers wrapped around the slender stem of his glass.

Emotion assailed her, too primal to qualify as sympathy, and far too complex to be dismissed as pity. There was such an isolation about him. He sat looking out across the water, so lost in dark thoughts that he was completely unaware of her even though she stood close enough to touch him. His hair lay thick and inviting, no more than a few inches from her hand. What would it feel like, if she were to riffle her fingers through it? How would he respond?

With annoyance, most likely! He wore his solitude proudly, a mantle designed to keep other people at a distance, and she'd be better off respecting that. She had no business wondering—*worrying*—about his feelings when it was her child who should be the focus of her concern.

She stepped forward, and the ring of her high heels on the flagstones alerted him to her arrival. "No," she said when he made to rise from his seat, "please don't get up."

But he ignored her and pulled out the other high-backed wicker chair. "Thank you for coming." He indicated the carafe and the second wineglass. "I didn't order this. The woman in the front brought it out as soon as she knew I was meeting you."

Nina shook the dark blue linen napkin over her lap and smiled. "Her name is Maria Torres."

"You know her well?"

"Well enough. She and her husband own and operate this place with occasional help from their children. The family came here as refugees from Guatemala just over four years ago."

Amusement chased the chill from his eyes. "When I said I was waiting for you, she checked me over so thoroughly, I thought she might ask for credentials to prove I was good enough to be seen with you. What have you done to deserve such dedicated affection?"

"I've had professional dealings with the family. Nothing too serious but, because of their refugee status, the family were terribly threatened by the legal process. They had visions of deportation and if ever they were sent back to Guatemala Señor Torres would face the firing squad. He was a very influential and outspoken critic of the regime there." She smiled again and raised her glass to him. "It's hard for us to imagine the sort of oppression that forbids a man the right to free speech, isn't it?"

"No," Hugh replied, and there was no longer the slightest trace of laughter in his eyes, or in the grim line of his mouth. "It's not hard for me, at all. No wonder the family treat you like their patron saint."

The chairs, softly padded with navy chintz cushions, invited relaxation. Nina leaned back in hers, schooling herself not to quiz him about his comment, or the reasons for this meeting. No doubt he'd speak soon enough. But he sat erect as a soldier, fingers drumming a tattoo on the glass surface of the table, the tension which had eased momentarily taking hold again with renewed force.

Maria Torres appeared, a tray loaded with small dishes of appetizers in her hands. "Señora Sommers, it is such a pleasure! I have *tapas* for you and the gentleman, special little things, fine and fresh from the market."

"Thank you, Maria. I'm sure they'll be wonderful. They always are."

Maria's beaming smile displayed an impressive row of gold-filled teeth. "For you, *señora*, nothing is too good or too much trouble!"

Once, the gratitude would have embarrassed her, but Nina had grown accustomed to it and knew how important such gestures of hospitality were to the Torres family.

Hugh, however, endured the interruption with ill-concealed impatience. "I've got to get Jane out of that house," he declared, the moment they were alone again. "I've still got doubts about the wisdom of moving in with you, but that's my problem, not hers, so if the offer still stands I'd like to take you up on it. I have a number of business calls to make while we're in the area that could keep me away for hours at a time and I don't want her to be left alone, day or night.''

"Not left alone? Then where...?''

"The couple who manage the complex offered to take her to a movie and keep her with them until I get home.''

"She didn't mind?''

"Being left with baby-sitters?'' He shook his head. "No. If anything, I think she was relieved.''

They were talking parental shorthand, anticipating each other perfectly with no previous experience. At any other time, Nina would have marveled. "But what happened?''

"What happened.'' He slumped in the chair and pinched the bridge of his nose between thumb and forefinger, seeming to forget where he was or that she sat perched on the edge of her seat waiting for him to answer.

"Hugh?'' Her voice coaxed him back to her. It was the first time she'd called him by name, and the way she said it, on a soft exhalation of anxiety, made it sound incredibly intimate. Good God, what was wrong with her, that she'd think a think a thing like that when something dreadfully upsetting had happened to his child? *Her* child! "Tell me, please.''

"There was someone in her room when she went downstairs to change after we got back from your place on Sunday afternoon. We're renting a four-floor town house, and the bedrooms are on the ground level. The sliding glass doors had been broken, and two men——''

"Good grief!'' Her response, sharp with concern, had other diners looking their way. "Were they—did they——?''

"She wasn't hurt,'' Hugh said, "but it was no thanks to me she survived unscathed. By the time I'd got my act together, they were gone and she was in a heap on the floor.''

"The poor kid! It must have been horrible for her." Nina's voice grew hushed. "For both of you."

Horrible? Yes! He closed his eyes, and recalled the whole thing, the details all the more vivid from being run through his memory yet again. How long had he stood there like a bloody idiot, thinking Jane was playing games with him, while she screamed his name, over and over?

It had taken the sound of a body falling heavily against a wall to spur him to action. By the time he'd raced down the hall that connected the two rooms, Jane was on her hands and knees, groping for the side of her bed, and all that was left of the intruders was the sound of their footsteps echoing down the treed lane that led to the underground garages and the main road at the end of the complex.

"Daddy," she'd whispered, dry-eyed and ashen with horror, "they went through all my things."

He'd scooped her up, overcome with remorse, stabbed with pity, weak with relief. But she'd been outraged.

Great dry sobs had wrenched her apart as she witnessed the destruction the intruders had wrought. Dressers and cupboards gaped open, their contents strewn everywhere. "They went through my drawers, Daddy," she'd gasped. "They touched my things!"

He hadn't cared. She'd felt like a bundle of twigs in his arms, as easy to snap in two as a matchstick, and all he'd known was a perverted gratitude that they hadn't splintered her with their violence. "So what?" he'd scoffed, in a clumsy attempt at comfort. "Things don't matter."

"They matter to me," she'd replied in a small voice. "They're my most important treasures." The observation had cut him to the quick.

Nina's voice wrenched him back to the present. "Was anything taken?"

"No."

"Did you phone the police?"

"No, ah . . . no. At the time——"

"Why didn't you call and tell me all this yesterday?"

"I don't—I hoped——" How did he account for his having taken this long to get his priorities in order? That only when he'd realized he was weighing Jane's physical well-being against his own emotional safety had he been shamed into taking any action at all?

"Never mind." She spared him having to explain, her voice husky with concern. "Listen to me, cross-examining you at a time like this! As if anything else matters as long as you're both unhurt. And of course my offer still stands. Pack up and drive out to the house tonight. I'll phone ahead and warn Sophie to expect you."

"It can wait until tomorrow. By the time we've finished dinner and Jane gets back from the movie, it'll be late. But thanks." He lifted his glass and took a hefty gulp of wine. "We're both grateful."

There was a tiny pause before she replied, "So am I." But it wasn't what she said so much as how she said it that made his stomach churn, partly from relief but a little from excitement, too.

Chalk up one more character flaw that, when all his attention should have been centered on Jane, he could interpret simple graciousness from a relative stranger as sexual promise. Reprehensible or not, though, there was no denying the magnetism that drew him to Nina. What

was it about her that made him want to abandon ten
years of caution and "go with the flow," as Jane would
say?

He liked to think of himself as a man persuaded by
logic. He had little tolerance for aging hippies with long
hair and unwashed feet who gathered in parks and
chanted about karma, but it suddenly struck him that
perhaps he tried too rigidly to control his own destiny.
Maybe, just this once, he should sit back and submit to
a superior power. It could hardly be worse than fighting
the current every step of the way.

He cleared his throat. "Well, now that that's taken
care of, I guess we can settle down and enjoy the rest
of the evening."

"Yes." She nodded. "When you see Jane, tell her how
relieved I am that she wasn't hurt, and also—er—please
tell her how pleased I am that you'll both be staying with
me."

He understood her hesitation. "I will," he promised,
and hoped that if he was prepared to run the risk of
finding the woman irresistible Jane would at least see fit
to recognize her merits as a mother figure.

They were sipping coffee and watching the last fuchsia
streaks of sunset fade into pale shell pink when Rolando
Torres appeared. Hugh had his back to the gate that
gave access to the sea walk and park beyond the
courtyard, but Nina saw the young man the moment he
emerged from the lengthening shadows of dusk.

Lithe as a dancer, he approached their table, his foot-
falls drowned out by the sound of guitar music playing
from outdoor speakers mounted on the stucco walls of
the restaurant. "Señora Sommers!" he exclaimed,
coming to a halt at Hugh's shoulder.

She had no time to reply, let alone make introductions, before Hugh reacted. He sprang up from his chair so suddenly that it flew over backward. Swinging around in a half crouch, he balanced on the balls of his feet and held both hands before him, lethal blades ready to slash at an opponent. Eyes narrowed to slits, he spoke rapidly in Spanish, his tone low and menacing. Although she didn't understand what he said, Nina had no doubt that he was prepared to kill in his own defense, should it be necessary.

Rolando danced out of reach, and raised his own hands in the universal gesture of surrender. *"Dios, señor!"*

In seconds, it was all over. Maria Torres hurried over, imploring forgiveness without bothering to determine the sin. Sensing the excitement was finished before it had properly begun, the other patrons picked up conversations where they'd left off, and Hugh shook his head as though to clear away the remnants of some ancient nightmare.

"I'm the one who should be apologizing," he said, relieving Maria of the chair she'd picked up and setting it back in place for her. "The boy startled me and I'm afraid I overreacted."

A mild understatement, Nina thought, noticing that although his hands appeared steady when he again picked up his glass he was about as relaxed as a cobra ready to strike. "This is Rolando Torres, Hugh," she said. "Maria's youngest son."

"It is all my fault," Rolando insisted gallantly.

Maria let out a little gust of relief. *"Sí!"* she wheezed. "He is a good boy, my Dito, but sometimes he is foolish. Children..." she flung up both hands and appealed to

Hugh, her smile uncertain " . . . we love them, but they make us old before our time, yes?"

Rolando slung an arm over her shoulder and squeezed her. "You're beautiful, Mama," he crooned, preparing to lead her back to her kitchen. "You'll never grow old."

Nina hid a smile. He had the face of an angel, the body of a young god, and the instincts of a kitten who badly wanted to appear a streetwise tomcat. He flirted with every woman who crossed his path. Some day, in the not too distant future, his charm would be formidable. Meantime . . .

"Señora Nina," he said, turning to face her once more, "there are matters we must decide. I have not forgotten my obligation to you, and——"

"I know, Rolando. Make an appointment to stop by the office and we'll work something out."

"*Gracias, señora.*" He nodded civilly at Hugh. "It was a delight to meet you, *señor.*"

"Hardly," Hugh muttered, watching mother and son disappear inside the building. "He must think I'm nuts."

Nina sipped her coffee while she thought about the best way to reply.

"Well, why don't you say something, instead of sitting there like the Sphinx?" The irony in his tone was underlined with belligerence. "You're wondering if you've got yourself mixed up with a lunatic, *sí*?"

With finely engineered precision, she replaced her cup on its saucer. "I'm wondering what makes you so defensive," she said evenly. "Or is what happened to Jane responsible for all this paranoia?"

The tension went out of him. "No," he said, reaching for the carafe and draining the last of the wine into his glass. "You just witnessed a conditioned and unfortunate reflex in an otherwise sane and reasonable man.

He came up behind me so quietly—that, and the Spanish.'' He shook his head, as though to chase away bad dreams. ''Sorry if I snapped at you. I don't usually make a habit of being such a jerk around my dinner dates.''

What sort of memories haunted him so relentlessly that he'd been ready to go for Rolando's throat with so little provocation? He looked solemn, his mouth unsmiling, and all of a sudden she wanted to kiss him, to feel his lips soften under hers and mold themselves into happier lines bent on private, wonderful exchanges between just him and her. Good Lord, she must have had too much sun!

''Is this a date?'' she asked, making a conscious effort to lighten the atmosphere a little.

But he turned those distant blue eyes on her so seriously that her smile faded. ''Definitely not! Tomorrow, I'm moving into your house. I'll be living with you for the next several weeks, partly for my daughter's safety, and partly because she needs the opportunity to get to know you better in case she ever finds herself with no one else to turn to. I can't afford to think of you as a date. I can't afford to think of you as anyone other than exactly what you are: the woman who, for reasons known only to herself, gave up a baby fifteen years ago and who now wants to make amends for those lost years. And you can't afford to recognize anything except that I'm taking advantage of you. We can be nothing but business associates, drawn together to achieve the successful completion of a very tricky project. Permitting anything deeper or more personal to develop between us could endanger everything we're trying to accomplish for Jane.''

So he felt it, too, that compelling electricity that arced between them despite its being entirely ill-suited to the situation in which they found themselves. Because, just as they'd spoken parental shorthand earlier, they cut corners now. She didn't ask what he meant, and he didn't try to explain. They both knew.

She was a fool to feel such a sense of loss over his rejection of something that had never actually happened. "I'm not a child, Hugh," she replied, delving into her bag for her glasses. "I learned the hard way how painful it can be to play with fire. You can move into my home easy in the knowledge that my hopes and expectations are entirely in sympathy with yours. I've waited too long to get to know Jane to take a chance on messing things up at this stage."

"I'm glad we understand each other." He went to pick up the small brass tray which held the bill folder and two mint chocolate wafers.

But she'd forestalled him by leaving her credit card with Maria when she first arrived. "No," she said now. "I've already taken care of this."

"That hardly seems fair, since I invited you."

"Business dinners are tax write-offs," she retorted with more sting than she'd intended and, popping her glasses on her nose, scrutinized the amount owing as closely as she knew he was scrutinizing her. Paradoxically, she felt less vulnerable behind the lenses, as though they threw up a shield he could not penetrate.

"Have I hurt your feelings, Nina?"

Yes! Whether or not it made any sense, he had!

She gave him the benefit of her most professionally astonished stare, the one she used in court to suggest that opposing counsel's conclusions fell so far short of logic as to be downright absurd. "Certainly not," she lied, pen poised to sign the Visa receipt. "I'm surprised you'd even ask."

But Hugh Cavendish was not opposing counsel and he didn't know he was treading on thin ice by pursuing the subject. "Then why do you look so crushed?"

It was that word, crushed, that revived her. "Don't be ridiculous!"

Signing her name with a flourish, she stuffed her glasses back into her bag and pushed back from the table, ready to make a beeline for the exit. The arrogance of the man enraged her. Poor Jane!

"I'll walk you to your car," he said, easily keeping pace with strides half again as long as hers.

"No need," she said tightly, shrugging his hand from her elbow and increasing her speed. "I'm perfectly capable of finding my own way without your help."

"Who's being defensive now?" he reproved her, half under his breath. "Stop pretending you're a racehorse, Nina, and smile. Your fans are watching and I don't want to get lynched in the alley for bringing a scowl to your lovely face."

The man was irresistible when he wasn't infuriating. Beguiled into a near smile, she muttered, "Oh, for heaven's sake!"

But he was right, damn him, and she'd have to learn not to let him get under her skin like this. If only he'd been born ugly or stupid or ignorant, or even a foot shorter than she, though, how much easier it would be to treat him merely as the liaison between her and Jane, and shelve all her silly inclinations to see him as the most appealing, romantic man she'd ever met.

"That's better." Laughter lurked in his voice and melted the chill blue depths of his eyes. "Now, since I do know how to behave like a gentleman when I'm in

the company of a lady, let me show off. Which way is
your car?''

Shutting out the disapproving voice of common sense,
she succumbed to his charm. They walked the short distance at a stroll, his step matching hers, and she wished
she'd left the car farther away, or that she could
reasonably offer to drive him back to his place—any
excuse to stretch the moment and make it last.

The air was heavy with summer, the sky a luminous
purple fading to lilac where the city lights flung up their
reflection. Horse chestnuts lined the street where she'd
parked, their branches meeting overhead in a tunnel of
dark, leafy green.

Across the road was a small park. A couple clung
together on one of its benches, totally wrapped up in
each other. Their lips touched, then the young man
whispered something that made the girl laugh huskily.

Nina looked away, appalled to find tears stinging her
eyes. For the first time in years, she felt envy. Had she
ever been that innocent, that carefree?

"What are you thinking?" Hugh asked.

"About not being young," she replied dolefully.

He chuckled, a sound as rich and warm as the night.
"You're not exactly over the hill, Nina."

"But I'm too old to believe in happy-ever-after. I think
I always was."

"I doubt that."

"It's true. I seemed to know from a very early age
that the higher one flew, the harder one fell. Sooner or
later, good times are invariably followed by bad."

"That's just the way of life, surely? Some ups, some
downs."

"I never saw it that way, then. It was more like being
punished for always wanting too much. I even re-

member the first time I came to that conclusion. It was my fourth birthday, and for the longest time I'd begged for a baby sister."

"Did you get one?" He sounded amused.

"No. My parents gave me a doll instead, and I absolutely refused to accept that it wasn't the real thing. It had hair I could comb, eyes that closed, and arms and legs that moved. It even cried and wet its pants. I was so determined it would grow into a real baby that I sat it on my swing, convinced it would hold on and enjoy the ride." She shook her head ruefully. "Of course, it fell face first on the ground, its pretty smile all smashed, and I ended up with neither a sister nor a doll."

"Fascinating." He leaned against her car and grinned down at her. "Tell me more."

"Why? Are you looking for traits in me that you saw in Jane at the same age?"

"I'm not thinking about Jane at all right now. I'm far too intrigued by you as a four-year-old, with huge, dark eyes and black hair." His eyes roamed over her face. "Were you as beautiful then as you are today?"

A blush flowed up her throat and over her cheeks. "I was unremarkable, except for being too tall for my age," she said, glad that the canopy of leaves overhead filtered the street lights and camouflaged her reaction to the compliment.

He leaned back farther, arms folded and hips snug against the side of her car. "I'm embarrassing you and I don't mean to, but I hardly think you were ever ordinary. Please tell me more about your childhood and this theory of yours."

She'd recite the entire Bill of Juvenile Rights if it would prolong the evening and the pleasure of his company, she thought, tearing her gaze away from the elegant length of masculine thigh stretched out in front of her.

"Well, the summer I was six, my parents took me away on holiday to a magical place of sunshine, white sand and warm blue ocean. I never knew just where it was—California, maybe, or even Hawaii, because I do remember it was the first time I traveled by air. Anyhow, while we were there, my father taught me to swim. I still have a picture of him straddling the waves, with me riding high on his shoulders and both of us laughing into the camera."

"So it was a happy time?"

"For a price, yes. That winter, he became ill."

How well she remembered her tall, vigorous father wasting away to a pale shadow of his once exuberant self, and her pretty mother growing pinch faced with sorrow. Nina had known without having to be told that she must be quiet in the house and not slam doors. She went to play in other children's gardens, but no one came to play in hers. People talked in hushed voices around her. She had known what was coming. "By the following summer," she told Hugh, "my father was dead, and something in my mother died with him. She became timid, and, to compensate, I became strong, the one she could lean on now that he was gone."

"I'm sorry, Nina. I didn't realize I was dredging up such painful memories."

"It was a long time ago," she insisted, despising the ache in her throat that made her voice grow thick. Pity was the last emotion she wanted to arouse in him. "In time, with just the two of us, things became better again. Not boisterously happy, the way it had been when my father was alive, but content. We weren't destitute. We had the house and all the good memories. There was a little money from an insurance policy, and people are generally kind to a young widow with a child.''

"Small compensation for losing a husband and father, I'd say.''

"It was enough, though. I felt safe in that sort of placid limbo—no great hopes, no great disappointments, you know? But eventually, my mother grew pretty again, pretty enough to catch the eye of the local bank manager, Gerald Corbin. He was dark and sober and cold. He thought children should be seen and not heard. He never picked me up and swung me high in the air the way my daddy had, yet, even though he seemed to hate the role, once he married my mother I had to call him Father.''

Get it together, Nina. You're being maudlin!

"You didn't get along with your stepfather, I take it?''

She stood a little straighter, reached for her car keys and pushed back the bitter memories. "That's another story. I should be getting home and so should you.''

He pushed himself away from the car with easy grace. "Will you be okay, driving all the way out to your place on your own?''

I've been alone almost all my life, she wanted to tell him.

Instead, she managed a laugh, a startled, rather breathless sound because, just before she opened the door and slid into the driver's seat, he caught her hand. His palm felt warm and dry, his fingers strong as they squeezed hers briefly. When was the last time a man had held her hand? When was the last time she'd met a man whose hand she wanted to hold? "Of course. I drive into town and back again every day, remember?''

"Be careful, anyway.'' His fingers squeezed again and then released her. "See you tomorrow?''

"Yes. We'll celebrate at dinner. To new beginnings."
Because it was the future that counted, not the past.
And because she was an adult now, mature enough that
she ought to have outgrown her childhood superstitions,
and surely wise enough not to build impossible hopes
around a man who'd made it plain that he'd come into
her life solely to take advantage of her.

Yet, when she stopped before turning the corner at
the end of the block and looked in her rearview mirror,
he was standing exactly where she'd left him, staring after
her and flexing the fingers that had touched hers—as if
the same prickling sense of shock was chasing over his
skin, the way it was over hers. As if he wanted to break
the rules he'd so firmly spelled out not an hour before.

Oh, Lord, this had to stop! The man would be living
in her home tomorrow, sharing meals and leisure time.
Lounging by the pool, with next to nothing on. Looking
at her out of those winter cool blue eyes and discerning
things he wasn't meant to see. Maybe touching her again,
casually or by chance. But all that was incidental to the
main reason their lives had coincided.

Nina wrenched her thoughts away from the secon-
daries and struggled to fix them on the main character.
Plain Jane, daughter of Hugh Cavendish, surely one of
the sexiest men God ever created.

*Help!*

# CHAPTER FOUR

A LENGTHY session in court the next day, defending lost, unhappy teenagers, restored Nina's priorities. She'd been handed an ideal opportunity to contribute something good to her daughter's life. It was all she'd ever really wanted, all that really mattered. She must do nothing to ruin her chances—especially not by imagining herself fatally attracted to the adoptive father. She'd been misled often enough in her early twenties to know better than to place much faith in the staying power of romantic infatuation. The unconditional love of a parent for a child was much more enduring.

She could hardly wait to get home, to find out how Jane liked her room and the rest of the house. Driving through the heavy traffic at the end of the day, Nina steeled herself to restraint. She wouldn't gush over the girl, she wouldn't gloat, and, no matter how tempted, she wouldn't touch. She would be matter-of-fact and calm, and on pain of death would she dish out unasked-for advice.

But when she entered the house just before six-thirty, the door to Jane's room stood open and it was more than Nina could do simply to say hello and keep going. For a start, Jane smiled at her with such unabashed pleasure that Nina found herself choking with emotion. Without so much as a twinge of guilt, she ditched her fine resolutions.

"Oh!" she exclaimed, stepping uninvited across the threshold and reaching both arms around to hug the girl fiercely. "I'm so glad you're here, and that you're okay!"

Just for a moment, Jane stiffened before submitting to the embrace, but it was enough to remind Nina that, already, she was helping herself to liberties she'd promised she wouldn't take. She stepped back and somewhat after the fact asked, "May I come in?"

"Sure." Jane gave an abrupt little lift of the shoulders that was uniquely hers, a gesture that she seemed to use indiscriminately to convey permission, approval or indifference.

Nina glanced around, taking in the clothes spread across the bed, the half-empty suitcases lying open on the floor, the odds and ends littering the little kidney-shaped dressing table. "How's the room?"

"It's super!" Almost as though she missed being held, Jane hugged her arms across her waist, cradling her elbows in her hands, and hunched her shoulders in delight. "My own bathroom, even, and I can go right out to the pool from here when I feel like swimming. And *that* over there——" she giggled, indicating a hundred-year-old *chaise longue* with a toss of her head that sent strands of hair flying out in a sun-streaked arc "—for when I want to act like a movie star!"

The urge to reach out and smooth her fingers over the unkempt bangs had Nina plunging her hands into the pockets of her tailored cotton shirtwaister. "It's a Victorian fainting couch," she explained.

Jane's eyes widened with awe. "I don't think I've ever fainted," she confessed, "but I had the wind knocked out of me on Sunday night. Does that count?"

Nina felt her laughter seep away, replaced by a frightening anger. What sort of men pitted brute strength against a fifteen-year-old girl? "Did they hurt you, darling?"

Jane's features seemed to flatten in an attempt to mask her feelings. "Nah," she said, swinging around to look out to the terrace.

She shouldn't have asked. She shouldn't have called her "darling." She shouldn't be in such a hurry to forge bonds. These were things that hinged on trust, and trust took time. "That's good," Nina said, trying to sound matter-of-fact. "We'll eat dinner in about an hour, so if you feel like a dip in the pool before then you've just about got time. Have you met Sophie, by the way?"

Jane nodded and twirled a strand of hair around her finger. "She lives here, too?" she asked, wandering over to the glass doors.

"Yes. She has a little apartment behind the kitchen."

"So that's your room then, next door?"

"That's right. And your father's in the guest loft above the garage. His windows look down on the pool, too."

The lock of hair coiled tighter, doubling back on itself under the tension Jane applied so ruthlessly. "So no one could get in without us knowing, right?"

The poor child was terrified under all that adolescent bravado. Well, to hell with taking things slowly! "No, darling. The entire property is walled and there's also an alarm system in place."

Jane's eyes flickered nervously. "Why? Have people broken in to your house, too?"

"No. Security measures are standard procedure in this neighborhood, that's all. And you'll never be left alone here, so please try not to worry."

Jane thought about that for a minute, her lower lip almost disappearing behind perfectly even teeth, then that endearing grin flashed again, almost as brightly as before. "Okay. Thanks for letting us stay with you, Nina."

Nina wanted to say how glad she was to have them, but the child's sweet honesty caught her by surprise and left her with her eyes suddenly swimming with tears. The best she could manage was an inarticulate gargle before she turned away and went blindly down the hall to her own room.

The same thing almost happened again about an hour later. They were gathered around the table in the dining room whose windows stood open to the warm evening air. Nina looked up from her salad, expecting to find two guests, and saw something else entirely. Not a man with Paul Newman eyes whom she wished she'd met at another time, not a gauche teenager disposed to unpredictable mood swings, but a family of three sharing dinner together. Out of the blue, the wonder of it slammed her heart against her ribs. A father, a mother. And their child.

The embarrassing tears sprang up again, but this time Hugh saw them and raised concerned brows. She managed a smile, a dismissive shake of the head. "Too much pepper," she muttered, disappearing behind her dinner napkin. "It happens every time."

Jane, demure in striped seersucker, edged Nina's water glass closer. "Have a drink," she advised, "and if that doesn't work, try the old 'arms up' routine."

Laughter bubbled over and saved her. Nina sipped water that tasted like champagne and tried to remember a time when she'd felt happier. It was a bit like coming out of a tunnel into bright sunshine, and looking behind into total darkness. An exaggeration, of course, and her vision would quickly adjust to reality, but for now she was captive in the brilliant warmth of the moment.

"My schedule's pretty flexible over the summer," she ventured. "If you like, I can arrange to take some time off to show you around the area."

Jane's shoulders jerked approval. "Okay." She giggled slyly. "Dad gets lost all the time, you know. We always end up some place we don't want to be."

"That's because I have a lousy map reader," he said, pretending disgust.

Her gamine grin teased him. "So teach me to drive, Daddy, then you can be the navigator."

"Janie," he sighed, rolling his eyes, "I'm already gray before my time. Don't force me into baldness, too."

"But bald is sexy, Dad."

He looked appalled, as though she'd uttered an unacceptable four-letter word in public. "It's *what*?"

"Sexy," she repeated blithely. "I read it in a magazine. A survey said that most women think bald men are sexy. Like Sean Connery, you know?"

"I know you're too young to read trash like that," he scolded her.

She made a face. "Oh, Daddy, you're so out of it sometimes! All the girls my age read stuff like that. We used to smuggle it into school all the time."

"Yes," he reminded her, "and look where that sort of behavior landed you."

Her expression turned sullen. "Why'd you have to bring all *that* up again?"

"Because you tend to push your luck."

"I had to do something to get out of that place," she complained. "It was worse than a prison."

"I doubt that, Janie," he replied with profound parental conviction.

But his certainty was short-lived. "Is she right?" he asked Nina later when dinner was over and the two of them had taken their coffee out to the terrace. Jane, good humor restored by Sophie's peach melba, had gone to set her room to rights and arrange her "things." "Am I out of it, when it comes to raising a daughter?"

"I think," Nina replied carefully, "that as far as people Jane's age are concerned, we're all out of it. I'm certainly no expert."

"Yet you've made strides with her since Sunday. I noticed right away. She seems to have accepted you at some level." He set his cup down on the patio table and leaned against the terrace wall, a tall silhouette against the night sky. "I was watching you at dinner," he said, then undermined all her poise by adding unexpectedly, "In fact, I could hardly take my eyes off you."

"Oh," she said, and sank into the sort of tongue-tied silence she thought she'd outgrown years ago.

He studied her in the dusk. She could feel his gaze flowing over her face, searching out secrets she wasn't ready to share, even with herself. "I think," he went on, the baritone voice sliding perilously close to a bass, "this arrangement of ours could lead to all kinds of complications. Are you prepared to deal with them, Nina?"

For a moment, she was tempted to be cute and ask him what he meant, but she discarded the notion. It might have been the clear-eyed candor she sensed in his regard, or the combined scent of potted tuberose and male cologne fermenting to hypnotic proportions in the heat of the night, that seduced her into boldness. "I'm trying to ignore them," she said, "but you're not making it easy, putting me on the spot like this."

"Oh, brother!" he exclaimed softly. "I can see we've got a problem. Two ostriches burying their heads in the sand, each hoping the other won't notice."

She dared to look at him again. "Is that what made you wait so long to call and tell me what happened to Jane?"

He shifted, linked his fingers and stretched both arms forward, palms facing out. "Yes."

"You really didn't want to come and stay here, did you?"

"No."

"Why not?"

"Because I don't want those complications I was referring to. In the last few months, I've had about all the problems I can handle."

"Then what persuaded you to change your mind?"

He made a sound halfway between a yawn and a sigh. "I like to think I'm a grown man, in control of my life. I could hardly justify exposing my daughter to the sort of danger she walked into, just because..."

Don't say it, Nina begged silently, wishing she hadn't asked. The awareness between them was already so vibrant that she could practically touch it. If he put the feelings into words, there'd be no ignoring them, whether they wanted to or not. "Well," she interrupted brightly, "at least Jane seems happy with the arrangement."

"She does, doesn't she?"

"And that's what really matters."

"Of course."

There was no moon, just a candle gleaming on the dining-room table and a million stars too far away to shed light. Sophie had finished cleaning up in the kitchen and had retired for the night. Miss Abigail Flint, who lived next door, was playing the piano, an old-fashioned love song that infiltrated the silence with melancholy sweetness.

Without warning, images filled Nina's mind. Of his mouth closing on hers. Of his hands shaping themselves along the curve of her spine and urging her against him. He neither moved nor spoke, but she knew with absolute certainty that he was aroused, and, to her horror, felt her own flesh soften in pliant invitation.

"Tell me about Jane," she begged with quiet desperation, and sought escape through the most killing topic of all. "Tell me about her mother. Your wife. What sort of woman was she?"

Tell me how wonderful she was, how much you miss her. Tell me no one can ever replace her, and set me free before it's too late.

"She was a bitch," he said. "I sometimes think that if she hadn't died I might one day have killed her. And she was my ex-wife for the last eight years of her life."

Nina reeled under the still-smoldering rage in his words. "Did Jane know how you felt about her mother?"

He'd been staring out across the dark waters of Georgia Strait, but at her question he turned his head sharply towards her. "Good God, I hope not! What sort of man do you think I am?"

Too complex by far, she decided, and so full of unresolved anger and regret that it was no wonder he was gray before his time. Yet, underneath all that, she sensed he was a gentle man, which made his controlled violence all the more shocking. He misunderstood her silence. "I suppose you're thinking you've invited a madman to live in your home." He sounded weary, as though certain that he'd put himself beyond the pale of law-abiding society with his honesty. "You're probably wondering if you're safe in your bed with someone like me let loose on the premises."

"No," she replied truthfully. Whatever else she might feel, she wasn't afraid of him. "I'm wondering why you married her."

"I thought she loved me for what I was," he said with such pained bitterness that Nina could have wept for him. "And I found out too late it was for what she thought I could give her."

"What was that?"

"Initially, babies," he said flatly. "I never knew a woman so obsessed with getting pregnant. And when she found she couldn't—I don't know, something changed. I thought, when we adopted Jane, that things would work out, and for a while they did. Sandra could push a carriage down the street, just like every other mother on the block. The thing was——" even all these years later, the bitterness seeped through "—I became more or less redundant, except as a provider. And no matter how much I tried to provide, it was never enough. Sandra was the most dissatisfied, insatiable individual I have ever come across."

"But she loved Jane." Aware that her purpose had backfired, that, instead of recalling hallowed memories, she'd resurrected nightmares, Nina searched for some redeeming feature about the woman. And failed again.

"She turned her into a possession, one she refused to share." He stared moodily at the sky. "And to my lasting shame, I let her get away with it."

A moth fluttered around them before stumbling toward the candle glow. "Which is why," Hugh went on, taking Nina by the elbow and steering her toward the open french doors, "I'm so grateful that Jane has the chance to get to know you."

He paused just inside the hall that ran the length of the house, and let his hand slide down to her wrist.

"You're what she needs at this point in her life, Nina," he murmured, his anger spent. "Please don't let her down."

Nina's heart turned over. Whether it made sense or not, his words and the look in his eyes made her feel brave enough to take on any challenge. Impulsively she slipped her hand around his neck, and drew his face close enough to kiss him on the cheek. "I won't," she promised.

He looked startled, as though he'd forgotten what a woman's lips felt like. Then he reached up to withdraw her fingers, and rested his mouth briefly against them before pushing her away. "Tell me to go," he whispered.

"Go." Before it's too late.

She watched until he'd crossed the terrace and she saw the lights go on in the guest suite over the garage, before she turned around and realized that it was already too late.

Jane hovered in the doorway to her room, her face a mask of hostile despair. "Honey," Nina said, hurrying towards her. "Your father and I were just——"

She was no more than a foot away when Jane stepped back and very quietly closed the door in her face.

The atmosphere at breakfast the next morning was thick with tension, as though a thundercloud hung over the house a storm about to break.

When spoken to, Jane replied with chilling economy, her manner so scrupulously polite that it was impossible to fault her. "No, thank you," she declined, when Nina offered her warm croissants and homemade raspberry preserves, and chose instead a triangle of dry toast. It was as if she meant to punish both adults by denying herself all things pleasurable.

"She saw, last night," Nina explained to a mystified Hugh, once the girl had finished her spartan meal and excused herself from the table.

"Saw what?"

A flush warmed Nina's cheeks. "You...and me." She paused, annoyed at feeling guilty about a gesture meant to convey simple gratitude and never intended to give offense. "When I kissed you."

His lashes swept down abruptly, hiding his eyes. "I see. That was unfortunate."

His response left her feeling more than ever as if she'd been caught in some cheap and steamy clinch. Ghosts that she'd believed had been firmly laid to rest years before rose up suddenly to confront her again. "*Trollop*!" "*Sinner*!" Her stepfather's accusations echoed down the years, no less outraged for having remained silent for so long. "*You have brought shame and disgrace to this house.*"

"I'll speak to her, if you like. Explain." Hugh's measured, reasonable baritone plucked her back to the present and consigned Gerald Corbin to the past where he belonged.

"No," she said. She was an adult, and fully accountable for her actions. She didn't need him or anyone else to intercede on her behalf. "That might make matters worse, as if we're trying to make excuses, or have something to hide." She risked a direct glance at those candid, topaz blue eyes of his. "We didn't do anything wrong, after all."

His gaze didn't flicker. "Not quite."

She met his look head-on without so much as a blink and persisted with the charade. "It would be best," she said, "simply to ignore the whole thing. That way, a minor incident won't get blown out of all proportion."

Disappointingly, he nodded and pushed back his chair. "You're right. Nothing of any importance occurred and it would be a mistake to suggest otherwise. Jane's inclined to overreact sometimes, but she recovers fast enough, especially if no one else pays any attention to her moods."

Sophie endorsed his opinion shortly after, when she came to clear away the breakfast things and found Nina staring morosely into the dregs of her coffee. "That Jane," she chortled, "she is not a happy one this morning. Ah, well, *c'est la vie*! Do not despair, Madame Nina. We will all survive."

Wise words, born of experience and rooted in common sense, but Nina discovered, as the week dragged by, that their validity was undermined by Jane's stubborn refusal to forget what she'd witnessed and get on with life. It would have been one thing if she'd been rude, or come right out and accused Nina of being more interested in Hugh than she had any right to be. Then, Nina could have defended herself.

Jane, however, was much more subtle. Outwardly a model child accepting her lot without complaint, she punished Nina for her transgression by looking through her with empty eyes and bestowing meaningless smiles that were little more than grimaces of distaste.

When there was no relief in sight by Thursday morning, Nina decided it was time to give common sense a helping hand before the whole summer passed in silent combat. She canceled her afternoon appointments and went shopping.

The house was empty when she arrived home laden with purchases. Hugh had gone into town for one of his meetings, Sophie was picking tomatoes from the vines growing on the south side of the garage, and Jane was spread out on a chaise next to the pool.

"There's something I want to show you," Nina called down to the girl, leaning over the terrace wall. "Will you come in for a minute?"

Rolling her eyes heavenward, Jane slapped closed her magazine, heaved herself to her feet and slouched inside the house. "Yes?"

"Go look in your bedroom."

Jane's eyes flashed indignantly. "You went snooping through my things!"

Whirling around, she rushed down the hall to her room. Following less hastily, Nina arrived on the threshold just as Jane discovered the shopping bags heaped on the bed. "What's all this?" she demanded, the truculence in her voice at odds with the flush of excitement she was helpless to contain.

"Open them and see." It wasn't the method she'd have preferred to use to force a truce, but Nina didn't care. Hadn't Sophie been the one, that first day, to declare that if the means justified the end anything was permissible in dealing with one's children?

Jane rummaged through the tissue paper in the first bag. "O-hh!" The bikini was hot pink bound with satin ribbon, and about as far removed from the shapeless black swimsuit as French designer elegance could take it. Jane held it up by its skinny little straps and exhaled a long sigh of pure pleasure.

"What do you think?" Nina couldn't help asking.

She had to admire the girl's restraint. Jane dropped the bikini on the bed with feigned nonchalance. "It's okay," she conceded. But her eyes adored it and she couldn't keep from stroking it with the tip of her finger.

"Well," Nina told her, "if it fits, it's yours."

Jane's eyes darted to Nina's face and away again. "Why'd you buy it for me?"

"Because as soon as I saw it I thought of you. Why don't you try it on? If you don't like it, we'll shop for something else."

It did all the right things for her, exposing her tiny waist, flattering her long legs, and bringing out the peach tones in her fledgeling tan. With studied indifference, Jane eyed the other bags. "Are they all for me, too?"

"Have a look, then you tell me."

"Okay." Jane gave her little shrug for the first time in days, and Nina realized how much she'd missed it.

There was another bikini, lime green with black parrots parading across it. Jane permitted herself a tiny squeal of joy when she discovered it. The full-skirted cotton sundress flared around her calves in a swirl of bright reds and blues. The mint green trousers and shirt brought out hints of jade in her eyes. But it was the lingerie that melted the last of her hostility. Dainty little undergarments designed to help a teenager bridge the awkward gap between childhood and womanhood, they were a beguiling mixture of frothy lace and smooth, cool cotton. Jane couldn't resist them. "I want to wear everything," she sighed, kneeling on the bed and sifting the fabrics through her hands, "all at the same time!" She looked at Nina, her face radiant. "Is it okay if I dress up for dinner?"

"Of course."

"This is one of the nicest things anyone's ever done for me." Jane shook her head wonderingly and then, on a final, subdued note, "Sorry if I've been acting rotten all week, Nina."

Nina reached out to smooth back the too-long, too-fine bangs on her daughter's forehead and, when her

touch wasn't repulsed, felt her heart grow whole again.
It had been bribery, plain and simple, but it had been
worth it.

Hugh, unfortunately, didn't see things the same way.
"What's all this?" he asked, when his daughter, colt-
ishly graceful in her sundress, raced into the dining room
just before Sophie served dinner. "I don't recall seeing
that outfit before, Jane."

"It's new," she admitted, with artless pride. "Nina
bought it for me, and a whole bunch of other clothes,
too, Daddy."

"Oh?" Frost glazed his voice. "Why? You brought
more than enough to see you through the summer."

"I wanted to do something nice for her," Nina said.
"Isn't that reason enough?"

"I suspect not, in this case. Stop galloping, Jane,
before you break something."

"Have you had a bad day, Daddy?"

"What makes you ask?"

"Your face looks all tight and old." She giggled, her
guard for once completely down and seldom seen impish
charm peeking through. "Pruney, you know?"

"No," he snapped deflatingly, "I don't. Nor do I wish
you to elaborate."

Jane's face fell. "I like my new clothes," she informed him, then added with unvarnished malice,
"They're *pretty*."

Nina saw the barb hit its mark and rushed to restore
harmony. "I thought that it might be nice to have wine
tonight. May I pour you a glass, Hugh?"

He fixed her in a stony glare. "It won't work," he
told her.

She glared back, resenting everything about him: his dictatorial tone, his high-handed attitude, and, most of all, the way he was raining on Jane's parade. "Exactly what do you mean?"

"Plying me with alcohol is not going to make it easier for you to manipulate me. It'll take more wine than you keep in this house to blind me to what you're up to, so I'll save you the trouble of wasting what you've got and tell you right now that not even in a drunken coma would I allow you, or anyone else, to subvert my authority."

He was jealous! Afraid she was trying to usurp him in Jane's affections! And was furious because he thought he ought to be above such petty weakness, even though he seemed to find it perfectly acceptable that she should flounder in uncertainty where Jane was concerned.

"Don't you think," she suggested calmly, "that you're arriving at some unfounded and hasty conclusions on the strength of rather flimsy evidence? In my experience——"

His smile slashed her composure to ribbons even before he spoke. "Your experience, counselor? *What* experience? You might be a damn fine lawyer, but unless you have other... indiscretions you've yet to disclose, your experience as a parent is so limited as to be negligible."

There was a tiny silence, so acute that Nina thought she could hear eternity ticking away. Then Jane moved ever so slightly, but it was enough to remind both of them that she was there and had heard every word.

Nina turned, and saw the wide, haunted eyes. Oh, *God*! she thought, and felt bitter waves of remorse rise in her throat.

"Is that what I was, an indiscretion?" Jane asked, in a thin little voice.

# CHAPTER FIVE

SOMEHOW, they smoothed everything over, at least superficially. "We're not talking about you at all," Hugh insisted. "We're talking about..."

"Priorities." Nina didn't know where she pulled the word from. It just surfaced above the dismay and anger that clouded her mind. How could they have been so careless, so insensitive?

"And good judgment," Hugh continued, his composure showing cracks also. "If people don't keep their priorities straight, they...they..."

"Commit indiscretions." Nina wanted nothing more than to put her arms around Jane, but was afraid to try. If the girl didn't object, the man almost certainly would, in his present frame of mind. "Your father doesn't think I exercised good judgment when I went shopping without first discussing it with him. I might have bought something unsuitable, something to which you might have...had an allergic reaction," she finished lamely, aware that she'd have been laughed out of court if she'd presented such feeble rationale before a judge.

"Well, I didn't," Jane replied with faultless logic, "so does that mean I can keep the clothes?"

"That's up to your father," Nina said.

Hugh wore the expression of a man much put upon. "Since they're a *fait accompli*——"

"What's that? Another indiscretion?" Jane pleated the full skirt of her sundress with anxious, possessive fingers.

72

"It means you can keep the damned things." He might have been spitting nails. "This time."

"Thanks, Daddy. What's for dinner? I'm starving!" Her sudden grin, and the question that followed, offered at least partial reassurance that Jane wasn't completely devastated by all that had taken place, but Nina felt as if she'd just been put through a meat grinder.

"Fried chicken, *ma belle*. Good food warms the heart as well as fills the stomach." Sophie appeared in the doorway, her face creased with concern, and Nina knew that she'd overhead every word that had passed among the three of them.

Dinner progressed. Jane devoured everything set before her. Hugh waded his way through each course, stonily taciturn except when he was being excruciatingly polite. Nina, too churned up inside to do justice to the food, pushed it around her plate and watched Hugh from under her lashes.

He'd been unreasonable and unkind, and she'd never forgive him for that crack about her indiscretions. How unfair that, even as she simmered with resentment toward him, she was still so impossibly drawn to him. Only a masochist would find herself attracted to a louse.

In any event, her obsession with the man would have to stop. The person who mattered the most was Jane, vulnerable and increasingly adorable. If, in order to win her daughter's affection and trust, Nina had to alienate Hugh, it was a price she was prepared to pay. Under no circumstances would she enter into power games with him. Jane was not a trophy to be awarded to the winner.

As soon as the meal was over, Hugh excused himself, obviously anxious to rid himself of her company. Jane followed shortly after, eager to rearrange her clothes closet. Nina, her anger feeding on itself the more she thought about what he'd said, wished that Hugh had chosen to remain. There were a few choice remarks she would have liked to direct his way.

She was debating the wisdom of paying him an unsocial visit when Sophie came in to clear away the dishes. "Do not grieve so, *madame*," she advised, touching Nina sympathetically on the shoulder. "What is done is done."

Nina sighed and rested her cheek briefly against her housekeeper's hand. "I can't believe we said such awful things, Sophie—and in front of Jane, yet."

"Children are tough, *ma chère*. They do not break as easily as we think."

"Even so, we ought to have known better."

"Tsk!" Sophie clicked her tongue and scooped up dessert plates. "One of the first things a wise mother learns is to forgive herself for being not perfect. We all make mistakes." She leaned over to extinguish the candles, then gestured toward the open french doors. "It is a beautiful evening, too fine by far to be wasted on regrets that will accomplish nothing."

She was right. A sliver moon peeped over the garage apartment, barely able to compete with the light spilling from Hugh's windows. Not a breath of wind stirred the hibiscus blossoms on the terrace. Far out to sea, fishing boats hovered like fireflies somewhere between shore and forever. The only sound was the musical splash of the waterfall as it poured into the pool.

She could stew all night and it wouldn't change a thing. Confronting Hugh when her own anger was barely under control would be a mistake; professional experience had taught her the value of a cool head when it came to winning a point, and only a fool would underestimate so worthy an opponent. Furthermore, when all had been said and done, one unpalatable fact could not be ignored: Hugh was, quite literally, in the driver's seat. If he so chose, he could pick up and leave town, taking Jane with him, and there wasn't a blasted thing Nina could do to stop him. Experience and reason notwithstanding, the knowledge left her seething inside. *Fulminating*!

"I'm going for a swim," she decided. "If anyone phones, Sophie, take a message. If it's really urgent, I'll call back right away, otherwise it can wait until tomorrow."

She needed to channel her rage into more productive directions and formulate new strategy, because it was not yet over between her and Hugh. He might think he'd had the last word, but she knew differently.

At first, she swam lengths with punishing speed, lifting her head to draw breath only when her lungs felt ready to burst. But the water flowed over her, warm and smooth as cream, sloughing away the hurt and blunting the edges of her anger. At last, the rhythm of her strokes slowed. Pleasantly tired, she ducked behind the waterfall and floated on her back, mesmerized by stars overhead that numbered in the thousands.

"Feel better?"

His voice intruded without warning, so close to her ear that she realized at once that he'd swum the length of the pool undetected, his approach masked by the mutter and splash of the waterfall.

"I was." He was beside her, dark and sleek, in the milk-warm water. With monumental self-control, she turned her attention away from him and back to the stars. "Until a moment ago."

He trod water, causing little eddies to swirl around, drawing her even closer. "I suppose," he said, his voice as deeply sensuous as black velvet, "you've been thinking about me and——"

Irritation stabbed her so fiercely that she might have been lying on a bed of stinging nettles. She flung him a brief, incredulous glare. "You wish!"

"—and deciding I'm a complete jerk. You're probably thinking that if I had a shred of human decency I'd apologize for insulting you the way I did."

"The thought did occur to me," she admitted loftily, "until I recognized I must be suffering some sort of mental aberration brought on by the heat, whereupon I dismissed the idea. Toads, as any right-minded person knows, never apologize."

Name calling? her legal conscience asked disapprovingly. Childish, Nina, and very unwise!

"This toad does," Hugh said, with melting sincerity. "I was way out of line, and I really wouldn't blame you if you told me to find some place else to stay."

"Don't tempt me!"

"I'm sorry, Nina. Truly sorry."

She never would have expected such humility from him. It took a big man to admit when he'd been wrong and, despite herself, she softened. She could afford to be gracious in victory. "Thank you, Hugh. Apology accepted."

"Good," he said briskly. "Now that that's out of the way, let's talk about your mishandling of Jane."

Nina's jaw dropped, and she almost choked on a mouthful of water. "I beg your pardon?"

"This business of your running out and spending a small fortune on a new wardrobe," he explained, as though she weren't fully in command of her faculties, "when she already has more clothes than she can wear."

"Having enough clothes and having the right kind of clothes are two different things."

At that, he grew so irritably defensive that she knew he'd already been through the same argument before, probably with Jane. "Are you saying there's something wrong with the stuff she's already got?"

"Yes." Nina folded her arms behind her head and stared at the tips of her toes floating just above the surface of the water. "They're dowdy. They look as if they came from the children's section of an outdated department store."

"What's so terrible about that? She's a child, isn't she?"

"She's halfway through her teens. That makes her almost a woman." She paused, contemplating the wisdom of trying his patience further, then decided that she owed it to Jane to be completely honest. Every other consideration aside, the girl's wardrobe was a fashion disaster, albeit neat and clean. "She needs clothes that reflect and flatter her emerging maturity, not things that point up her ungainliness. You said once that she isn't a very happy person. I think a lot of that stems from the fact that she doesn't feel good about herself, and, at that age, looking good and feeling good are very closely related."

"Hogwash!" he replied, scornfully. "You're just trying to gloss over the real issue, which has more to do with your need to win Jane's approval than it has to do with her so-called emerging maturity."

Under cover of dark, Nina flushed. "Oh, really?"

"Yes, really. You bought her forgiveness, Nina."

"So what if I did?"

"That's not the route to take," he chided, ignoring her defiance as if she were a fractious and not too bright child. She could have throttled him, for his avuncular charity *and* for being right. "You leave yourself wide open to being blackmailed by her every time she wants something or doesn't get her own way. I told you, give her enough time and she'll come around without your having to resort to bribery."

Nina flipped over to face him, treading water the same way he was. "Time is the one thing I don't have on my side, don't you see? If I can't win her affection in the next six or seven weeks, I'm history. It's different for you. You can afford to be patient and you've got the rest of your life in which to practice the acceptably proper methods of bringing up a daughter. I don't. I have to take shortcuts."

"Affection that has to be bought isn't worth anything, Nina."

Right again, damn him! "Then what *does* make it worth something?"

The air swirled with the scent of roses and nicotiana; with traces of her perfume and his after-shave, Chanel marrying perfectly with sandalwood and musk. He inched closer, so smoothly the water barely rippled. "This?" he rumbled, his breath winnowing over her eyelashes and down her cheek to find her mouth.

And then he kissed her. Not violently, not aggressively, not even possessively. Just tenderly. Breathtakingly.

With the touch of his mouth on hers, all those dearly held romantic fantasies that she'd relegated to the intellectual limbo of her mind sprang free, their penance served. Her lips softened, accommodating the stealthy passion of his.

She tried to feel outraged. He was hardly playing fair, after all. But this was one time when her emotions refused to pay heed. The kiss deepened, the tempo changed. He explored her mouth. And she did more than merely acquiesce. She invited him in.

His hands came up to cup her face, tilting her jaw to keep her head above the water, while below the surface his legs stroked powerfully, brushing against hers, and keeping them both afloat. It was as well he did. She was drowning in different depths and had no energy to spare.

How could a kiss transmit such power that she felt it in her breasts, in the pit of her stomach, even in the soles of her feet? How was it possible that he discovered so much about her without their once exchanging a word? How did he know what her body craved?

He closed the distance that separated them and brought his chest firmly against her nipples, intuitively answering their aching plea to be touched by his warmth. He slid one hand down the length of her spine until he found the dip of her waist. Then his arm curved around to pull her hips forward.

And he was there. Aroused. Waiting.

Quickly, before he stole more than she could afford to lose, she tore her mouth free and drew in a shaking, painful breath. "Hugh...please..." she begged, then, realizing that what she meant and what she'd said weren't quite the same, she amended the plea. "Please, don't."

"Why not?" His voice was almost as ragged as hers.

"Jane might see, and——"

"She can't." The fingers of his other hand whispered down her neck to hook themselves under the strap holding up her swimsuit. He tugged, gently, remorselessly. "We're hidden behind the waterfall. No one will know."

He was right. They were quite alone, quite concealed. He could safely strip her naked. Except...was this what it was all to be about? Sneaking around and hoping not to get caught, like naughty adolescents who'd just discovered sex?

Oh, surely not! She, at least, knew how fleeting that sort of pleasure was. If ever she allowed herself to become sexually involved with a man again, it would be for the right reasons and it would be with the dignity such intimate commitment deserved. She was too old and much too wise to think she could again live without her self-respect.

"But I would know," she said, "and so would you."

He heard the conviction in her voice and, to his credit, he honored it, even though she knew his flesh was in an uproar, as was hers. "You're right," he conceded on a long, resigned sigh, "but, oh, Lord, Nina, how I wish you weren't."

He did the gentlemanly thing and reached down a hand to help her out of the pool. Not that she needed assistance. She was as graceful as a mermaid in the water and perfectly able to manage by herself.

She picked up her towel, murmured good-night, and walked away without a backward glance, which was just as well. He had no wish to be caught gaping and drooling like some clod who'd just found out that women were built differently from men. But what it cost him to let her go!

He shook his head, hoping to clear his mind. He'd noticed her quite by accident, happening to glance out of his window just as she sliced neatly into the deep end of the pool. And he'd been hooked, no more able to ignore her than a starving man could walk away from a feast. Out of his clothes and into his swimming trunks in about thirty seconds flat!

Of course, he'd told himself he was obliged to join her. He *did* owe her an apology—hell, he'd have decked any guy who'd mouthed off at him like that! But she also had to be set straight on a few things concerning Jane, and the pool had seemed as good a place as any in which to do it. At least they'd be alone if another shouting match developed.

Drops of water ran into his eyes, blurring his last image of her before she disappeared inside the house. Impatiently, he swabbed them away with the back of his hand, then raked his fingers through his hair to keep it from dripping down his face. He'd been in such a hurry to talk some sense into her before she finished her swim that he'd forgotten to bring a towel with him.

Talk *sense*? He shook his head again, mockingly this time. When had he started lying to himself? The first time he'd seen her, when he'd stood in the gazebo and watched the way she stalked toward him with the aloof, elegant grace of a pedigreed racehorse? The first time he'd seen her in a swimsuit, and realized that her legs, from ankle to thigh, were a masterpiece of elegance matched only by the rest of her?

Or was he focusing on the irrelevant to avoid having to face up to a more subtle and much more dangerous truth? One that went straight for the gut, like a fist slamming the wind out of him. One he hadn't even begun to suspect until they first looked each other in the eye. Suddenly, he swore loudly, a scatalogical vulgarity that he hoped never to hear cross Jane's lips. It had taken him forty years to get what he thought he needed to be happy: worldwide acclaim by other professionals in the field of geotechnical engineering, enough money to feel secure, and the satisfaction of knowing he was at last doing a half-decent job as a father. Too old by about twenty years to believe in bolts of romantic lightning striking out of the blue.

Nina Sommers was all wrong: wrong type, wrong style, wrong temperament. *If*—and it was a big *if*—he ever got involved in a serious relationship again, it would be with a nice, placid woman who wanted nothing more than to warm his bed, iron his shirts and make a home for him and Jane. And if that labeled him male chauvinist in spades, it was just fine with him.

He certainly did not need a rich, opinionated female lawyer who made him crazy, and whose nit-picking legal mind had long ago figured out that if she snagged him she'd get what she really wanted without any hassle: namely, Jane. And if that made him paranoid and insecure in the eyes of other people, too bad! He was certainly past the age where what the rest of the world thought mattered a damn to him.

There would be no more schoolboy fantasies about a leggy goddess transformed into a mermaid with her dark hair streaming halfway down her back and her skin pearled by starlight. No more tormenting himself with how it would feel to make love to her until her eyes turned hazy with passion and she forgot it was not socially correct to cry out his name and beg for more. It would be eyes and hands off from now on.

Of course, he would be civil; sociable, even. He was a guest in her home, after all. But he would never again allow himself to forget that she had no relevance in his life, only in Jane's.

Nina was busier than she'd expected for the next three weeks. It seemed that the extended heat wave brought out the criminal element in adolescents who'd led hitherto blameless lives. Maybe the long, warm evenings were a factor, making the streets and parks more attractive than home. Maybe people left house and car windows open to catch a breath of air. Whatever the reasons, she had a rash of phone calls requiring her mediation in cases ranging from petty theft to vandalism and, according to the probation officers with whom she dealt, there were plenty more to come.

Not at all the sort of person who enjoyed seeing young people in trouble, she nevertheless welcomed the need for her services. It left her with virtually no time to think about the near disaster in the pool. Bad enough that she and Hugh had resolved nothing, without her having to dwell on the complications they'd managed to create. Professional obligations gave a valid reason for her to leave the house before he appeared for breakfast in the mornings, and for her to be gone all day. If there was no avoiding him in the evenings, she made sure Jane was present also, and concentrated all her attention on her daughter.

That, at least, was no hardship. Contrary to what Hugh had so gloomily predicted, Jane showed no sign of trying to take advantage of Nina's generosity. Instead, she seemed more willing to confide her thoughts than she had been before.

"How come you understand so much about kids?" she asked, one evening when the three of them were sitting on the pergola outside the living room. "Most people don't even try to know about us, let alone care."

It was the sort of remark that went straight to Nina's heart, bypassing all the moments of sullenness and inexplicable moodiness that were part and parcel of living with a teenager. "I guess," she said, "it's because I spend so much time with kids your age, and also because I remember so well how it felt to be fifteen."

Something must have shown on her face, because Jane looked at her curiously. "You hated it as well, huh?"

"It wasn't the happiest time."

"How old are you now, Nina?"

Hugh, whom they'd both thought to be absorbed in his newspaper, lifted his head and leveled a reproving glance at his daughter. "Don't be cheeky, Jane."

"I'm not," she said. "I just wondered how old she was when—well, you know..."

"When I got pregnant with you?" Nina finished for her.

Jane shrugged, the familiar gesture that Nina would always associate with her daughter at fifteen. "Yeah."

"Well, to answer your first question, I'll be thirty-two at the end of September."

Jane chewed on that for a minute. "So," she decided at last, "you were only a bit older than I am, when it happened?"

"Yes."

Another pause, slightly more momentous. "Was it horrible? Being pregnant, I mean?"

It was a straightforward enough question, yet the reply was fraught with difficulties. How much easier to be completely truthful and say that it was the most terrifying, shocking ordeal she'd ever had to face. And how potentially damaging to Jane's already fragile self-esteem. Yet how could a responsible adult minimise the enormity of such an experience? "It was...frightening, I suppose."

"I bet you wanted to get rid of me."

"Get rid of you?"

"Yeah—you know, have an abortion."

Nina had been intensely aware of Hugh throughout the whole conversation but, if Jane had forgotten, his reaction to her last remark served to remind her that he was present and listening in with both ears. "What the devil do you know about abortion? It's not a subject someone your age should even be familiar with."

"A girl at school had one last year," Jane announced calmly, "and after she'd had it she came back and told us about it."

Hugh looked thunderstruck. "Is that what I was paying hefty school fees for? To have you primed with that sort of sordid information?"

"She was a friend and needed to talk to someone. It's called 'venting her anxiety.' Her psychiatrist said so."

"Then let her talk to her psychiatrist," Hugh declared. "That's what he gets paid for. And you'd be better off remembering you're judged by the company you keep, and start choosing more desirable friends."

Nina drew in her breath, wondering how he could possibly not realize the inevitable direction the conversation was taking. "Sometimes——" she began.

But Jane was too pink cheeked with indignation to remember not to interrupt an adult. "She's a nice girl, Dad!"

"Nice girls don't get pregnant," Hugh ordained, and gave his paper a peremptory shake to indicate the matter closed.

Jane was not deterred. "Nina did," she pointed out.

He inhaled sharply, beside himself with irritation. "Nina was different."

Nina decided she was tired of being discussed as if she weren't able to speak for herself. Jane was gaining the upper hand in a debate whose outcome offered no clearcut answers. As for Hugh, he was already knee-deep in a swamp of trouble and still didn't know enough to look out for alligators underfoot. She wasn't about to let him wriggle so easily out of the tight spot in which he found himself. If he didn't yet know the pitfalls of issuing sweeping generalizations as if they were immutable truths, it was time he learned.

"I was not different," she contradicted, her tone daring him to disagree. "I was a nice, ordinary girl who made a mistake. It's something that can happen to the best of us."

"See!" Jane's eyes flashed triumphantly. "You don't know everything, Dad."

Jane, Nina decided, sometimes did not use the brains she'd been born with.

"Apparently I don't." Hugh's baffled glare swung from his daughter and settled on Nina. A muscle twitched in his cheek and he tightened his grip on his paper as if he wished it were her throat. "Perhaps some time you'd care to enlighten me and explain, if you can, how nice girls manage to wind up in so much trouble."

The self-righteous ass! Had he been born perfect, or was it something he'd had to work at?

She glared right back. "I'd be glad to, any time you're prepared to hear me out before you decide to condemn me."

"I want to be there," Jane informed him. "This concerns me, too."

"You've pushed your luck far enough for one evening," Hugh warned her. "If Nina chooses to tell you the story of her life as it pertains to you, that's up to her and you. What she and I have to discuss is not necessarily the same thing, and you are not invited to be present."

"That's not fair!"

"Fair or not, that's the way it's going to be," he told her.

Jane appeared to debate the wisdom of arguing further, then settled for flouncing out of the room. Hugh immediately turned his attention back to Nina. "If I don't unwind, I'm going to get a lousy night's sleep. What do you say to a long walk along the beach? You could use the time to broaden my education."

"Now?" She hadn't expected him to be so anxious to take her up on her offer. She'd thought he'd at least give her time to prepare herself. Didn't he know she'd be baring the most private details of her life to him, and trying to do so honestly at the same time that she won his respect, if not his sympathy?

"Why not?" he asked immovably. "Unless, of course, you're afraid to be alone with me."

She winced. "Why on earth would I be afraid to be alone with you?"

He smiled, a tight, unamused little grimace that left his eyes cool and watchful. "That's something else you can explain to me," he told her, tossing aside his paper and stretching. "Especially in view of the pains you've taken to avoid me recently."

# CHAPTER SIX

THE tide was far out, leaving great pale sandbars exposed to the moon. They were the color of oyster shells, and smooth as a dance floor. Nina carried her sandals and walked, barefoot, a little apart from Hugh, keeping track of the distance that separated them by watching their shadows marching ahead.

They had not spoken a word since they'd left the house, and the silence, not comfortable to begin with, hung oppressively between them.

"It's a pity we missed the sunset," she said, and wondered what on earth people would find to talk about in times of stress, were it not for the weather.

"Tell me about it."

She stared at him, surprised. "The sunset?"

"Don't be obtuse," he said, not deigning to spare her a glance. "How the hell did you manage to get yourself pregnant at fifteen?"

There it was again, the accusing voice of virtue! "The same way I'd have managed it at twenty-five," she informed him tartly. "How do you think?"

She knew he looked at her then, because she saw the shadow of his profile etched sharply on the sand and turned her way. And she felt his anger. It scorched the side of her face. "Damn it, don't be flippant with me, Nina! Who was he, an older man? A neighbor?"

"No," she told him, belatedly realizing that he was looking for reasons to defend, not condemn, her. Suddenly, she wished she *could* blame someone else, and almost hated him for making her feel ashamed of something she'd paid for years ago. "He was a child, like me. We were in the same class at school."

Hugh's shadow seemed to sag. "So you knew what you were doing?"

"No," she said, looking beyond the shimmering waves to another horizon. "I only knew that I was desperate for love."

"Why didn't you go to your parents for it?"

"Don't you think I would have, if they'd had any to give?" she cried, a pain she thought she'd forgotten surging up so acutely, it snatched her breath away. "Or is it just that you think I was a tramp? If you do, you're in good company. That was my stepfather's exact reaction."

His shadow loomed closer, and one arm reached for her. "I don't think that! I'm just trying to understand, that's all. Were you and the boy going steady, or...?"

She flinched away from his touch. "It wasn't a one-night stand, if that's what you're asking. We'd dated a few times, and I liked him. I think he liked me. We even fooled ourselves, for a little while, into believing that we loved each other."

How it all came back, the sense of alienation from her mother, the hurt, the need to be close to someone, to have someone care enough to hold her in his arms.

"It might be important to let Jane know that she was conceived in love," Hugh suggested.

Conceived in love? Hardly! Where had love entered into a union that had more to do with loneliness than desire, with misery than with joy?

"Don't try to glamorize it, Hugh, or absolve me of blame. My stepfather always justified his tyranny by claiming he was cruel now to be kind in the long run. I tried to vindicate what I'd done by using the same line of reasoning in reverse. It was the here and now that mattered, not the consequences nine months later."

Without permission or warning, Hugh grasped her hand and gave it a squeeze. "What did you do when you realized you were pregnant?"

"I wanted to die," she said, hanging on to him as if he were the lifeline that kept her connected to the safety of the present while she delved into the past. Somehow, his touch made it easier to be brutally honest. "Because it was then that I discovered the most dismaying truth of all: that all kinds of things masquerade as love, making the real thing hard to recognize and even harder to find."

Oh, God, how shabby it all seemed in retrospect: the awkwardness, the blind fumbling in the back seat of the parked car. And the embarrassment, the fear that someone might see.

She swallowed. "Do you know how it feels, to share a secret with another person and be so ashamed of it that you can't look him in the eye? To realize that he feels the same and would like to pretend he doesn't know you?"

His grip on her hand tightened. "Oh, yes. In the end, that's what my marriage came down to. Avoiding each other's eyes, pretending the other one wasn't really there. It was the only way to get through the days. As for the nights——" his laugh was bitter, a splash of acid on the perfect watercolor of the evening "—the nights don't bear talking about."

For a while, they walked in silence, each one nursing private wounds. When they started talking again, it was about inconsequentials, a local jazz festival, a cocktail party for a retiring Supreme Court judge that Nina had to attend the next evening. And always, the weather. How hot the summer had been, how much the gardens needed rain.

Then, out of the blue, Hugh asked. "Did he beat you? Your stepfather, I mean."

"Not often, and never in a rage or on impulse. He'd strap me across the leg or the wrist with his belt, but he always prefaced the ritual by telling me that it hurt him more than it hurt me. Then, he'd count the strokes, being meticulously fair not to exceed the prescribed number."

"*Bastard*!"

"He was an extremely controlled man. I think that was what disgusted him the most: that, despite his excellent example, I'd shown such a lack of discipline in my fall from grace. He'd have found it so much easier to be charitable if I'd been the victim of rape."

Hugh thought he heard a quiver in her voice, and looked at her to confirm the suspicion. It was a mistake.

At dinner, she'd worn a loose white dress made of some sort of thin, filmy stuff that floated around her whenever she moved and merely hinted at the body beneath. When they'd decided to walk on the beach, she'd changed into jade green shorts and a matching top that left her midriff bare and showed a great deal of olive-tinted skin. Her hair, tied back with some sort of scarf, hung darkly halfway down her back. Moonlight washed over her, turning her into a delicate shading of triangles and curves, from her cheekbones to her breasts.

He slid his hand up her wrist and felt the fragility of bone. He looked down, past her hips to the incomparable elegance of her legs.

He thought about a man wielding a belt.

"Is your stepfather still alive?" he asked, and wondered how the words squeezed past the tightness in his throat.

"No," she said, and even though the night was warm he felt her shiver.

"Good. Because if he were I'd kill him."

He hadn't felt such savage frustration since the day they'd thrown him in that stinking jail cell in Colombia—with one vital difference: he was a free man now, and the woman beside him was only an arm's reach away.

He didn't forget that he'd sworn never to touch her again. It simply ceased to be important. All that mattered at that moment was that he somehow find a way to bring her back to him. Because, even though she'd presented the facts dispassionately and without a trace of self-pity, she was the prisoner of memories that he'd insisted she resurrect, regardless of the pain they caused her, and it was now up to him to free her.

"Nina," he said, and turned her toward him so that he could put his arms around her and hold her tight.

At first, it was enough. She leaned against him and pressed her face into the curve of his shoulder, drawing on his strength and taking the refuge he offered. But then she moved, lifting her head so that she could look at him, and opening her lips to speak. And before he knew his own intent, he'd brought his mouth down on hers.

Just a brief kiss, he vowed silently. And might as well have promised to rearrange the stars.

He took her by surprise. He always had, right from the beginning, bewildering her with contrasts: his chill reserve that hid such passion; his arrogance that melted into a humility that touched her unbearably. Sometimes, she thought he was the loneliest man she'd ever seen, his eyes the light and distant blue reminiscent of snow shadows—until he smiled, and then they filled with warmth and a dry, intelligent humor.

None of that, though, was any excuse for lingering in his embrace now, savoring the texture of him. But how he beguiled her with his long, silky lashes casting shadows over the ridge of his high cheekbones. With his lips, deceptively cool and gentle, and his tongue, hot and hard and aggressive. He tasted of salt air and summer, of coffee and sun-ripened nectarines, all laced with hunger for a different kind of nourishment.

When he'd first pulled her to him, she'd wrapped her arms around his waist, grateful for his understanding. She'd had no intention of allowing her emotions to run wild. But they did, though just when insanity displaced reason she didn't know. One minute, she was leaning against him, the way she might have leaned against a sympathetic brother; the next, she was welded to him, frantic with a hunger not about to be easily appeased.

Somehow, his shirt had ridden partway up his back, exposing a section of smooth, tanned ribs covered with just enough flesh to madden her and, before she knew it, she was out of control, running her hands over him, her sense of touch so vibrantly alive that she could almost feel where the tan line ended just above his narrow hips.

He wooed her without mercy, sending cadences of passion crashing through her bloodstream. And suddenly, after all these years, her heart knew it wanted him to be the one to wipe away those old, imperfect memories; wanted him to override the habitual caution that sometimes left her feeling so barren and old.

How nice it would have been to be free to indulge desire. And how impossibly it would complicate things!

She willed herself to move away. Yet her feet resisted, her arms clung, and her eyes shut tighter as if, by refusing to admit a crack of moonlight, they could deny the passing of time.

Still her brain nagged. Not here, not now, not him. You made the rules, now stick to them.

He might have heard. "Enough!" he muttered against her mouth, and practically shoved her away. "Keep your hands to yourself."

Outrage rushed in to heat the appalling cold that prickled over all those parts of her that had stolen warmth from him. "You kissed me first!"

"You kissed me back—and then some!"

"Oh!" She scrubbed her mouth with her hand. How could a man so well versed in the art of seduction be so lacking in chivalry? How could he be so brutal?

He tugged at his shirt, stuffing it back inside the waist of his trousers, then ran the fingers of both hands through his hair. "Don't say it," he warned. "I know I'm a crass, insensitive oaf. I'm also a man, not a saint, and if you don't want me to fling you down on the sand and take you, in full view of anyone who might happen to stroll by, then quit being such a tease."

"I wouldn't lower myself," she retorted, saw the grin he couldn't quite contain, and realized too late her unwitting pun. She stood a little straighter and drew offended silence around her like a cloak.

"Hey!" His voice cajoled her. "It was my fault, okay? I started things. Give me credit at least for having the good sense to stop them, too. Quite apart from any other consideration, this is hardly the place for two respectable adults to be groping around, tearing at each other's clothing.''

Her face flamed. He had a bad habit of stating the truth baldly, and of being right more often than he was wrong. "I know. I'm sorry, too."

He caught her fingers companionably in his and swung them back and forth. "What were we talking about, before I got us off track?" he asked, turning her around and strolling back the way they'd come.

"Gerald Corbin, my stepfather."

He grimaced. "Of course. How could I have forgotten?" He flung a glance her way. "Do you want to tell me the rest, or is it too painful?"

"It's painful," she admitted, "but I might as well finish, now that I've started. If I can make you understand why I chose the options I did, I might even be able to forgive myself for what I had to do."

"It strikes me that you're not the one who should be seeking forgiveness. Where was your mother in all this?"

"A silent minority, kept firmly in the background where she belonged," Nina said, old bitterness souring her words. "She didn't have the courage to oppose Gerald."

"What did he do, throw you out of the house?"

"That would have been the kind thing to do. Instead, he tried to set what he saw as my ruined life back into some sort of order. He condescended to let me live at home, even though it meant bringing disgrace on the family, and at first I was frightened enough of the consequences of what I'd done to be grateful. But then he decided that, since my obvious lack of moral conscience made me unfit to be a parent, he and my mother would adopt my baby and take responsibility for its upbringing."

"Good God!"

"Exactly. I think it was at that point that I made a great leap from childhood to adulthood and decided to take control of my own life. I went to stay with my aunt Laura, who was my father's older sister and also my godmother. I'd sort of lost touch with her over the years, but she welcomed me as if I were her own and never once judged me."

"And your mother let you go?"

"Don't feel sorry for me," Nina said, pulling her hand free. "My mother made her choices and I made mine. We all do what we have to do, and she threw in her lot with Gerald Corbin the day she married him. In my case, I had to go through a pregnancy and a birth knowing that, at the end of it all, the only choice I had was to place my baby for adoption so that she had the chance for a decent life with people who wanted her and loved her for her own sake, and not because they wanted to win the admiration of the whole community for their so-called Christian charity."

"You're right. You had no other choice." Hugh's voice was husky.

"No, I didn't. I was too young to bring up a child alone. I had neither money nor the education to earn it, and my godmother, although willing to support me for as long as I needed her to, was by then well into her sixties and no longer a young woman. She didn't need the stress of a baby underfoot all the time." Nina didn't mean to draw in a long, ragged sigh. It just emerged. "People who break the rules have to pay a price. Mine was hearing my baby's first cry and never getting to hold her."

"That was a bit harsh, surely?"

"It was the way things were done back then. I knew she was healthy, and that was all. Before I left the hospital, I signed the consent papers for the adoption, and the only other contact I ever had with the social agency who handled the case was when they wrote to tell me that she'd been placed with a family."

"Oh, to hell with keeping my distance!" Hugh exclaimed, and hugged her to him again, resting his chin on the crown of her head. "I can't stand listening to all this and not holding you. I guess I never really wanted to think about the fine print involved in giving up a child. It was easier just to accept Jane as the gift she was, and ignore what it cost some stranger to give her away. But now that stranger is you, and that changes everything."

She pushed him away. "I don't want your pity. I was held accountable for my behavior, and if that was painful people like my stepfather would say it was no less than I deserved."

"I'm not entirely convinced people should always necessarily get what they deserve," Hugh said, as they approached the stairs that would take them to the path that led up to the house. "I know society has determined that the punishment fit the crime, but there are some circumstances that warrant a little more kindness, especially if the people involved are too young to bear such severe consequences."

"I agree. That's why I decided to specialize in juvenile law. A lot of teenagers make mistakes, but they're not necessarily criminals and shouldn't be treated as such."

He looked a bit doubtful about that, and changed the subject. "Everything you've told me, about Jane's birth and all, happened a long time ago. I don't mean to belittle the experience or anything, but why haven't you had other children?"

"In case you haven't noticed, I'm not married. And if you're thinking that didn't stop me the first time," Nina said coldly, "then I suggest you rearrange your thoughts."

"Don't be so damned silly!" he scoffed. "That's not what I'm thinking, and you know it. Why haven't you married?"

"I was engaged once, and came close enough to marriage to pick out a wedding gown."

"And?"

"The dress didn't fit. It was long, made of white silk with seed-pearl appliqués, and sweetly virginal. Not suitable at all."

"Couldn't it have been changed, then?"

He had obviously missed the point.

"Oh, yes, but my past couldn't, and the man I once thought would make such a fine husband decided he couldn't live with the secondhand model who'd be wearing it. 'Too shop worn' were the words he used, as I recall. He had rather high social ambitions, and I suppose he thought I'd be a bit of a hindrance with my murky past. He was also insanely jealous of poor Bobby Griffiths."

"Who was Jane's natural father, I assume?"

"My 'ex-lover,' according to my fiancé," Nina corrected him, and heard a totally unplanned giggle ripple out of her mouth.

Hugh looked rather startled. "Why is that funny?"

It wasn't, not really. Merely ludicrous.

"Because," she said, sobering up, "poor little Bobby Griffiths was as inexperienced as I was, and practically needed a guidebook to figure out how to kiss me. 'Lover' conjures up an image totally at odds with the way he really was."

"I see."

Nina was sure he didn't. Only someone who'd been through the same sort of experience could understand how the emotional pain and scarring so far exceeded the price that should have been paid. There had been no pleasure and precious little romance in the loss of innocence, for her or Bobby.

"What about other men, after the fiancé backed out?" Hugh persisted. "Or did you decide at that point that there were more important goals than getting married and settling down to raise a family?"

"Such as what?"

"Being successful. Making money," he said. "That minimansion up there on the hill must have cost you a few dollars."

"I inherited that minimansion from my godmother, along with most of the furnishings and a sizable sum of money," Nina informed him, a dangerous edge to her voice. "Would you like to know my bank balance, as well as how many lovers I've had?"

"Don't be so prickly! You're a beautiful, rich woman. I'm sure you've remained unattached by choice, and I wonder why."

"Because the older I get, the choosier I become. There are plenty of attractive, available studs around. Good men, however—the kind a woman wants to keep over the long haul—are scarce as hen's teeth."

"So are good women," he retorted, then, after ruminating for a minute, went on in a tight voice, "I suppose you're going to this Friday-night cocktail party with one of the many attractive *studs* you mentioned?"

"No," she shot back, "I'm not, but what interests me is why you ask. Do you want me to invite you?"

"Yes," he said irritably. "I do. How formal is it, what time do we have to leave, and do you think Sophie would mind baby-sitting Jane?"

He was jealous!

Nina raised her eyebrows and cast a glance at the man in the moon, who seemed to be wearing a distinct grin. "Semi, seven, and you'll have to ask her," she said, and wondered how she kept her own face straight.

The next day, Rolando Torres came to see Nina at her office, to finalize his arrangements to look after her garden for the rest of the summer as part payment for her having represented him in juvenile court two months earlier.

"And in the meantime, Rolando," she warned him, tapping her pen on the file in front of her, "try to stay out of trouble. This was your third appearance before Judge Burke. He's running out of patience."

"Señora Sommers!" Her name rolled off his tongue like honey. Liquid eyes beseeched, elegant shoulders lifted expressively. "I was in the wrong place at the wrong time. Those people were not my friends and I knew nothing of their plans to rob the corner store. I was there only to buy milk for my mother."

"I believe you. Fortunately, so did the owner of the store. Next time, you might not be so lucky."

"There will be no next time," he promised.

She smiled. It was hard not to around Rolando. "How's the bike? Will it be able to handle the distance to my place without breaking down in the middle of the highway?"

Mention of the old British Norton which he'd rescued from the scrap heap and lovingly restored had Rolando beaming. "If you saw my baby, *señora*, you would not need to ask. She gleams, she purrs, she is wonderful!"

"Good." She peered at him over the top of her reading glasses, and tried to look severe. "Then you'll have no excuse for not showing up on time when you're supposed to."

He placed a hand solemnly over his heart. "On my honor, *señora*, I will be at your door at ten o'clock in the morning, starting this weekend, without fail."

# CHAPTER SEVEN

AT HALF-PAST nine on Saturday morning, Nina joined Hugh and Jane on the terrace for a leisurely breakfast, unsure of the sort of reception she'd get from Hugh. The cocktail party the previous evening had not been an unqualified success.

He was hidden behind the morning paper, with Jane sitting across from him, her face sullen. "If you won't listen to me, listen to your girlfriend," she pouted, as Nina slid into place at the table. "Tell him, Nina. Tell my father that if he doesn't want to be bothered spending time with me I'm old enough to be left on my own."

"My spending an evening with Nina does not make her my girlfriend, Jane, and she doesn't influence my decisions regarding you." The paper lowered long enough for Hugh's cool blue eyes to acknowledge Nina briefly. "Good morning."

"And a beautiful British Columbia morning to you, too," Nina replied affably. "Is there a problem?"

"No," Hugh said.

"Yes," Jane said. "Do you know how totally insulting it is for you two to go out partying, and leave me with Sophie, as if I'm a baby?"

"I don't understand. I thought you liked Sophie," Nina said.

"She wouldn't let me watch *Teenage Bride of the Vampire Prince*," Jane complained, "and, on top of that, she made me go to bed at ten-thirty."

Hugh's voice floated up smugly from behind his paper. "That's why I left her in charge."

"*Now* do you understand?" Jane sighed, appealing to Nina.

At that moment, Rolando's Norton roared up to the back gate next to the garage. "Good God!" Hugh exclaimed. "What's that?"

"My temporary gardener has arrived," Nina told him.

The paper lowered once more, just as Rolando let himself in the gate, motorcycle helmet dangling from one hand, black leather jacket half unzipped. "I repeat, what's that?" Hugh said.

Nina reached for the coffeepot and filled her cup. "Surely you remember him? You met him the night we had dinner at his parents' restaurant."

Hugh adjusted his sunglasses. "Now that you mention it, yes, I remember very well."

"I thought you might. Jane, would you like another Danish?"

Jane wore the expression of someone locked in a trance. "No, thank you," she replied, reaching for a cherry twist without taking her eyes off Rolando, and aiming it vaguely toward her mouth. "What's his name?"

Hugh frowned. "What's he doing here?"

"Rolando." Nina directed her attention first at Jane, then at Hugh. "I already told you. Gardening."

"Rolando who?" Jane wanted to know.

"Why?" Hugh asked.

"Good grief!" Half annoyed, Nina set down the coffee pot and surveyed the pair of them. "What's the big deal about a boy weeding a few flowerbeds?"

"If you needed someone to tidy up the garden, you could have asked me," Hugh said, reproof implicit in his tone.

"I don't expect house guests to earn their keep," Nina replied coolly. "Besides, Rolando and I have an arrangement. He owes me a little favor."

"Oh?" Hugh looked more disapproving than ever. "How so?"

"A business matter and it's private, so please don't cross-examine me any further. He'll be working here for the next couple of weeks, and that's that."

"That's very unwise, if you ask me."

"I'm not asking you," Nina informed him, thoroughly ticked off by his attitude, "so please don't get yourself all bent out of shape."

Hugh's eyes took on a glacial sheen. "Any more orders, or are you through for today?"

"It's very boring," Jane announced, "sitting here, listening to adults fight all the time."

"Then don't listen, *ma petite*," Sophie advised, appearing from the kitchen with a bowl of fruit and a fresh batch of pastries. "Come into the kitchen and learn how to bake a cake."

"That sounds boring, too."

"More so than cleaning your room?"

"I want to work on my tan." Jane, Nina noticed, was gazing at Rolando as if he were a vision.

"You will look fifty when you are only thirty if you cook your pretty skin so much. The cake," Sophie suggested, "is a much better idea, but..." she shrugged "...what do I know? Only that my bread is burning in the oven, and that this young man looks as if he could use a little snack."

She beamed at Rolando, who had discovered a rake in the garden shed and stood waiting politely in the background.

"Sophie," Nina said, smiling at him also, "this is Rolando Torres, whom you've heard me talk about. Sophie is my housekeeper, Rolando, and if you haven't put on weight by the time you've finished working here it won't be her fault. She's a magnificent cook, like your mother."

Rolando offered Sophie his most charming smile. "*Señora*," he murmured, and kissed her hand.

"Good God!" Hugh snorted, and rattled his paper.

Nina ignored him. "And this is Jane, who's spending the summer with me."

"*Señorita*." Rolando gave a little bow.

Jane promptly turned bright pink and hid her hands with their chewed and mangled cuticles. "Hi," she croaked.

Sophie took charge. "So, first a snack, and then work," she decreed, urging Rolando toward the kitchen and waddling after him like a mother hen shooing her prize chick back to the coop.

Jane watched them go. "I think I'll change my mind and learn how to bake a cake, after all," she decided, wiping cherry jam off her chin and jumping to her feet.

"Sit down!" Hugh barked. "You don't charge away from the table without permission, and in any case——"

"Please may I be excused?" She looked at Nina.

"Yes, sweetheart," Nina said. "Have fun with the cake."

The silence following Jane's departure was short-lived and intense. Hugh's paper, cracking against the table with the velocity of a rifle shot, brought it to an end.

"You," he spat, rage simmering, "are on very thin ice, Nina Sommers, and I've had just about enough!"

Nina took her time selecting a peach and a cluster of black Ribier grapes. "That sounds almost like a threat to me," she said conversationally. "I do hope I'm mistaken."

"You're not. It is. Keep up this...this usurping of my authority, and I will put Jane safely out of reach of your influence which I'm beginning to think is not the kind to which a young, impressionable girl should be subjected."

Nina yawned delicately, a calculated gesture to mask her anger. "Temper tantrums are so unattractive in a man of your years, Hugh. What brought on this latest?"

She could almost hear him grinding his teeth. "You gave Jane permission to leave the table."

"A socially acceptable thing to do," she replied, "and one it is my privilege to offer, since I'm the hostess."

"I don't want her in the kitchen."

"Why not? I think it's commendable that she's interested in learning to cook."

A flush further darkened Hugh's deeply tanned skin. "She's not in there because she wants to learn domestic arts, and you bloody well know it. She's in there because of that boy. You saw the besotted look on her face when he showed up."

"Well, that's hardly his fault, and, in any case, they aren't alone together. Sophie's there, too."

"A fat lot of good she'll be!"

"That's not what you thought last night when you entrusted her with Jane's safety and well-being," Nina pointed out.

Hugh's expression tightened. "Last night," he said darkly, "Sophie had only a movie to contend with. Now, she's got the Vampire Prince in the flesh!"

Nina tried to quell the laugh, but it rolled up from her feet, gathering force every inch of the way, and exploded merrily out of her mouth. "Hugh, I think what's really bothering you is that you've just been presented with firsthand evidence that your little girl isn't so little any more," she gurgled, all her anger swept away, "and you're having a hard time adjusting to the idea."

"What father wouldn't, with someone like him hanging around?"

He was not amused, not even slightly. It took a little of the sparkle out of the day. "Rolando is a charming, good-looking boy. Sooner or later, one was bound to catch her eye, and, since even you can't stop the progress of time, be glad it happened here where we can keep an eye on the situation."

"Be glad?" Hugh echoed, his voice rising.

"Yes. In case you haven't noticed, Jane's been getting restless. She's spent the last month entirely with adults and she's missing being around people her own age. A bored teenager spells trouble. I think Rolando showed up at just the right time. He'll be good company for her."

"That...? With my daughter? He's got a gold ring in one ear, for Pete's sake. He wears his hair in a ponytail. He rides a motorbike." Hugh's indignation grew to a final crescendo. "If he owes you a favor, it means you've had to represent him in court. He's a bloody criminal!"

"No, he's not, Hugh," Nina said, her patience wearing dangerously thin. "If he were, he'd be in jail."

"The only reason he isn't is that you went to bat for him, and got him out of one mess after another. He *should* be in jail! Then, at least, I could go about my business without worrying that he's corrupting Jane's morals when my back's turned."

"Are you saying that I perform a public disservice with my work?" Nina asked with ominous calm. "Or is it my character in general that you hold in such low esteem?"

"It's your job to try to get kids like him off the hook, and I'm not faulting you for being good at what you do," he allowed generously.

"How magnanimous of you. I'm overwhelmed!"

"*But*," he cut in, her sarcasm making about as much impression as a gnat on a warthog's hide, "you become too personally involved with your clients. Your judgement becomes clouded. You convince yourself that hoods like this Rolando are poor, misguided victims of a harsh and unforgiving society that refuses to understand them."

"And I suppose," she said, tossing her napkin down on the table, "that you understand him perfectly on the strength of your very brief acquaintance with him?"

"The facts speak for themselves, Nina."

"What facts?"

"He's been in trouble with the law," Hugh stated without a tremor of uncertainty and, when she didn't refute it, went on, "Hasn't he? Admit it, Nina. The kid's been in court more than once, and you got him off the hook each time. No wonder his parents think you hung the moon!"

"All right," she snapped. "He's been in trouble a couple of times."

Hugh slapped his hand on the table with satisfaction. "I knew it! He's got a record as long as my arm."

"I said trouble, Hugh, not prison, not even reform school. Rolando is small potatoes compared with most, and he's making a real effort to wipe the slate clean. Give him a chance!"

"You sound just like that idiot at last night's party!"

"Ah," Nina said, leaning back in her chair and folding her arms. "I wondered when we'd get around to last night. Which particular idiot did you have in mind?"

"Barney." Hugh mimicked the man's rather affected drawl so perfectly that Nina almost smiled. "The one who equates touching and feeling with conversation. The one with the new BMW."

"You amaze me, Hugh. I thought you'd like him, you have so much in common. He's the prosecutor's chief assistant and usually the man opposing me in court. If he had his way, every juvenile guilty of the slightest misdemeanor would be behind bars."

"If he's the best the court can come up with, then it's no wonder you manage to get all your clients off."

"Why, thank you! What a charming thing to say."

Hugh had the grace to look a little ashamed. "I don't mean it that way, Nina. I know you well enough to respect your intelligence, even if I don't necessarily agree with your opinions. But Barney BMW, with his flabby handshake and moussed hair, is the kind of guy I can do without—obsessed with what he owns, how much money he makes, and so busy casing every woman in the place to decide which one'll be his next acquisition that he can't string two words together and make sense."

Nina winced. Oh, dear, he had Barney pegged, all right! She, too, had often wondered how so bright a lawyer could be such a social boor. It was as if he left his brains behind in court at the end of the working day.

"He spent half the night undressing you with his eyes," Hugh added sourly. "Not that he had to work very hard. That blue thing you wore barely concealed your front and made no pretense at all of covering your back. I'm surprised it didn't fall off!"

"That was a pure silk Fiorella jumpsuit, and very securely held up by a halter strap."

"It was outrageous, and if your reason for wearing it was to make sure every man in the room got an eyeful you certainly succeeded."

"Is that why you were so antisocial, because you disapproved of what I wore? Or because other men besides yourself noticed?"

Her eyes were dancing, flecks of silver lurking in their basalt depths, and she had a little smile on her lips that infuriated him. He was jealous as hell, and she knew it!

Oh, he'd spent too long in the far-flung outposts of civilization for sure, if controlling the sort of primitive reactions he'd experienced last night was beyond him. He'd thought he was in charge of his life, and it enraged him to discover that he could fall afoul of such petty nonsense.

The evening had been a disaster from the outset. First, there'd been that outfit of hers to contend with. Just as well they'd taken his car and he'd done the driving. It had kept his hands where they belonged. Then had come the setting: golf and country club at its most exclusive, with guests so self-consciously rich and successful that it left a bad taste in his mouth reminiscent of his married days.

He hadn't needed the aggravation of suspecting that every other man there was panting to snuggle up to Nina's cleavage. To be fair, she hadn't shown all that much of it. It had been more a matter of his imagination working overtime over what lay hidden that had had him in an uproar. What with the admiring looks directed her way and the covert envy aimed at him, it had added up to a bit more than he'd been able to handle equably.

Again, though, he couldn't exactly fault her. Standing tall and proud in spike-heeled silver patent sandals that brought her to within three inches of his height, she'd responded with supreme indifference to the effect she might be having on anyone else. Her eyes had smiled into his the whole night, even when she was engaged in social chitchat with other guests. She had looked marvelous, smelled heavenly, and he'd wanted nothing so much as to take her outside to where dark velvet fairways lay deserted beneath the stars, and slide his hands inside that alluring top.

He hated how she affected him! Hated the fact that not once, in all the years that he'd been married to Sandra and had thought they were reasonably happy together, had jealousy lanced through him because of the way other men looked at his wife. The implications of such a conclusion were disturbing, to say the very least.

Nina was supposed to make life easier, not complicate it beyond redemption. Yet here he was, his thoughts off at a tangent from the real issue of Jane's welfare, and all because he couldn't keep his mind on any topic for more than a minute at a time when Nina Sommers sat across from him, long limbed, smooth skinned, and glowing like amber in the morning sun. And to top it off, he was fighting another of those bloody headaches. Would they never cease?

Exasperated with the whole world and especially himself, he snatched up his paper again and dived behind it, away from that knowing smile, away from that face that paraded through his mind far too often, especially when he slept.

"I've got to run a few errands in the village," Nina informed Hugh about an hour later. "Is it going to offend your sensibilities if I take Jane with me?"

"You don't make a very good bitch," he shot back, "so drop the sarcasm, okay? You know full well I'd far rather Jane spent the afternoon with you than hanging around here watching Romeo pull weeds."

She acquiesced with a slight shrug. "Are you planning to be here for dinner?"

"Yes," he replied nastily, "but if my presence is beginning to weigh too heavily you'll be glad to know I plan to be away for most of next week."

That did it! "You know, Jane's quite right. It is very boring when two adults bicker like children all the time. Do you suppose we can call a truce and try to enjoy the rest of the weekend?"

He tossed down the pen he was using to fill in the weekend crossword and pressed a hand to his temples. "Sorry."

"Have you got a headache?" she asked, a shade more sympathetically.

"I've got a hangover," he corrected her ruefully. "It's my punishment for being such a jackass."

"But you didn't drink very much last night."

"No, but Manhattans never did agree with me."

"Well, lean back," she ordered, going to stand behind him, "and rest your head against me."

"What for?"

He sounded so suspicious that she laughed. "I'm not going to throttle you, even if you do deserve it! How does this feel?" She massaged his temples, kneading in small circles from the tips of his eyebrows and up into his hair.

"Wonderful," he groaned. "Where did you learn such a technique, or shouldn't I ask?"

"My father used to do it for my mother when she had migraines. After he died, I took over the job. I guess it's a bit like riding a bike—you never forget how it's done."

She knew from the increased weight of his head at her waist that he was beginning to relax. "You have magic hands," he murmured.

He had magic hair, so alive and thick that it seemed to cling to her. She wanted nothing more than to run her fingers through it and arrange its random waves into some sort of order. It must have curled all over his head when he was younger, but he wore it short enough now that it behaved itself most of the time.

What had he looked like at twenty, before the black had been dusted with silver? Devastatingly handsome, no doubt, with the contrast of those topaz blue eyes and that dark skin, but surely not more arresting than he was at forty? There were lines on his face now that gave him character and told the story of his life: pain and laughter, sorrow and joy. It was the strong, intensely masculine face of a survivor.

His eyes were closed, their absurdly long, straight lashes untouched by the gray that streaked his hair. She liked him this way, with his soul shut away from her.

She could look her fill without being touched by the loneliness she so often sensed in him, or feeling threatened by the passion that lurked in those cool depths, then blazed into icy fire when she least expected it.

From old habit, her fingertips swept past his ears, searching out hidden points of stress, and quite by accident discovered a narrow ridge beneath the thatch of his hair. Bending lower, she separated the strands so that she could inspect it more closely, then wished she hadn't. A pink swath of skin, about the width of a pencil line, curved from the base of his skull to just above his left ear. It was a wicked looking scar, and not very old. The sight of it hurt her somehow, and left her feeling quite sick. Backing away a pace, she clapped a hand to her mouth.

"What's the matter?"

With a start, she realized his eyes were open and he was watching her. "This scar," she began, her voice sounding thin and a little hoarse. "It's so...cruel. How did it happen?"

"It's a long story."

"I don't mean to pry." But she did want to know.

"Sometime I'll tell you about it, but not now." When he closed his eyes this time, it was not the same. A frown puckered his forehead, as though the headache which had begun to recede was back with renewed force.

"Why don't you stretch out on one of the chaises in the shade, and let me get you something to relieve the pain?"

"Thanks," he said, "I think I will."

She brought him aspirin, a pitcher of homemade lemonade, and an ice pack.

"You're a good woman, Nina Sommers," he murmured, touching her hand. "Remind me of that the next time I get miserable with you."

"You can count on it." He was pale under his tan, and a vein throbbed visibly just above his eye. "Will you be all right on your own?"

"Yes. I'll sleep it off in an hour or so."

She pushed away the temptation to fuss over him. He was a grown man, able to look after himself, and she was a fool to delude herself into believing he wanted her by his side. "Well then, I'll be on my way."

Before she could move, his lean, tanned fingers tightened around her wrist. "One more thing. I need to ask a favor. About my being away next week—it's business. I'm flying up north to visit a proposed dam site. Not exactly the best place for a fifteen-year-old girl, so I wondered...is it all right if I leave Jane here with you?"

What elegantly masculine hands he had, she thought inconsequentially, her mind in such an uprush of emotion that for a moment she couldn't formulate a coherent reply.

He misinterpreted her hesitation. "Does that pose a problem, Nina?"

"No," she rushed to assure him, her voice choked with something that felt perilously close to tears. "I would be absolutely thrilled to look after her. It's just that I'm so surprised and delighted that you'd trust me with her, especially after everything we've said to each other, this morning."

"Trust isn't something I'm very good at."

"I'm beginning to realize that and I promise not to let you down. You have to know how much I've come to love Jane, and that I'd cut off my right arm before I'd let anything hurt her."

"Don't get carried away," he said, his mouth turning up in a faint smile that she found irresistible. "I sort of like your right arm. Just keep an eye on . . . that situation with the Torres boy."

"Please don't worry. Whatever you might think about Rolando, you know that Jane has good instincts, and by now you ought to know that I have, too."

"In my book," he returned dryly, "instincts fit somewhere between trust and intuition. I tend to regard all of them with a rather jaundiced eye."

"Will you feel better if I back them up with solid, twenty-four-hour supervision, and promise that Jane'll never be left alone with Rolando?"

"I'll feel better. Now get going on your errands before the whole afternoon's wasted."

"I thought I'd bring back fresh crab for dinner. Do you think you'll feel up to cracking shells?"

He leaned back and closed his eyes again. "If my skull doesn't crack first."

She wanted to press her lips against that pulsing vein, touch them softly to his eyelids; whisper that she was worried about him, that she'd miss him this afternoon, next week, and whenever he wasn't with her.

Out of nowhere, she suddenly wanted to tell him how much she loved certain things about him. She said, "Then I'd better be off. I'm supposed to be getting my hair cut in fifteen minutes."

"Don't get it all hacked off." One blue eye opened and squinted at her. "I like it long. It's your crowning glory."

# CHAPTER EIGHT

NINA thought having Jane to herself for almost a whole week would be the most wonderful thing in the world, and it was, except for one flaw. Somehow, without Hugh there also, the pleasure was oddly incomplete.

Heaven knew, it shouldn't have been like that. The days were never long enough to do all those things she'd always promised herself she'd do with her daughter if she ever got the chance. They shopped exhaustively, nothing terribly expensive because the last thing Nina wanted was to upset Hugh again, but they had fun poking around in the little boutiques in the village, and finding new and interesting places to eat lunch.

The good weather held. Every afternoon after he'd finished working for the day, Rolando would sit outside the kitchen door and sip a tall glass of Sophie's home-made lemonade before riding his Norton back to town. And every afternoon, Jane would maneuver things so that she was there in time to join him.

True to her word, Nina supervised the visits, albeit from a discreet distance. She really had no reason to hover over the young pair. Apart from the fact that Sophie's vigilance never flagged, Rolando treated Jane with such gallant respect that Nina felt it would be insulting to eavesdrop on every word they exchanged. Not for the world would she have done or said anything to dim the radiance of Jane's infatuation. The girl glowed from the inside out.

But, along with the glow, came the classic symptoms of dissatisfaction with her appearance. "Long hair is *so* boring," she lamented, wrestling with her knots and tangles one morning. "At least, on me it is."

It was the opportunity Nina had been waiting for. "Why don't you have it cut a bit shorter, then?"

"It wouldn't change anything." Jane stared at her reflection in the mirror. "How come I'm so ugly, Nina, and you're so pretty?"

A spasm of pain contracted Nina's heart. "Oh, sweetheart, you're not ugly!"

"Yes, I am." Jane examined her face dispassionately. "I know what I can see."

"We're going out," Nina decided, seizing her chance. "There's someone I want you to meet."

"What do you think, David?" she asked her hair stylist, when they paid him a visit an hour or so later. "Is this the face of an ugly young woman?"

He flicked his comb through Jane's hair, rearranging it away from her features. "It's a face half hidden by bangs. How can I possibly tell? But from the little I can see, I'd have to say no. Skin so fine and clear could never be called ugly. I know women who would pay a fortune for such a complexion. The hair, however..." He rolled his eyes dramatically. "The hair is a disaster, sundamaged, split at the ends, and badly in need of styling. But there's lots of it and, with the right cut, it could be wonderful."

Jane chewed her lip uncertainly. "How short do you think it should be?"

"Short." David was emphatic. "Such a well-shaped head and pretty ears deserve to be shown off." He snapped his fingers at one of his assistants. "A shampoo and conditioner for the young lady, Roberta, then we'll experiment.''

The transformation was miraculous. All that fine, unmanageable hair, grown suddenly biddable as David sculpted it along more disciplined lines, revealed secrets about Jane that no one had suspected. She bore a resemblance to Nina after all, especially around the cheekbones and jaw. She had lovely brows and those eyes, which had so often seemed furtive peering out from her curtain of hair, appeared much larger and greener without their camouflage.

"I can't believe it!" she exclaimed, gazing in the mirror at her new image.

"Neither can I," Nina admitted. "You look beautiful, sweetheart."

"No," Jane replied judiciously, turning her head from side to side, "I just don't look ugly any more. Do I really have pretty ears, Nina?"

"The best!"

More lip chewing followed, then, "Do you know what I always wanted, more than just about anything else in the world?"

"What's that?"

"Pierced ears, with gold hoops like yours, only bigger."

How uncomplicated her ambitions, and how easily satisfied! Nina thought wistfully. When she'd been that age, she'd wanted so much more. "Would you settle for a bit smaller, at least to start with? Gold sleepers are usually quite tiny."

Jane's face lit up. "You mean, I can have them done? Today?"

"I don't see why not——" Nina stopped, wishing she'd been less impulsive as a thought occurred to her. "Unless you think your father would object?"

"Do *you* think it would be okay?"

"Yes, but it's not up to me."

"Well, he left you in charge, and you're my mother, aren't you?" Her eyes, clear hazel and shining with hope, impaled Nina through the mirror.

At the question, the maternal craving Nina had lived with for years almost tore her in half. How, after waiting all her adult life for the chance, could she deny it satisfaction when it was finally offered? "Yes, darling, I'm your mother."

"So," Jane slanted a gamine grin at her, and twirled the styling chair on its pedestal, "you decide . . . Mom!"

Wisdom, foresight, good old-fashioned common sense, what chance had they against such blandishment? Nina shut her mind to the possible recriminations Hugh might heap on her when he returned. "We'll get them pierced. Today."

Jane bounced out of the chair with more alacrity than grace and hugged her. "You're terrific, Nina! And don't worry about Daddy. He won't mind a bit."

On Friday evening, the weather broke. A summer gale came howling in across the Pacific, flattening everything that got in its way and causing a power failure that left whole neighborhoods in darkness.

All sorts of anxieties flitted through Nina's mind. Why couldn't the rain, so badly needed, have fallen gently instead of lashing down in wind-driven torrents? Hugh's flight was due to arrive shortly before midnight. Could the plane land safely in such conditions? Would it be delayed? Canceled? Would the endless hours between now and his arrival here, at the house, never pass?

Jane's thoughts were occupied elsewhere. "It's so romantic," she sighed, helping Sophie light candles. "I wish Dito was here."

"Dito?" Sophie inquired.

About to go over to the garage apartment and leave a supply of candles for Hugh, Nina stopped. "Is there something I ought to know?" she asked, wondering what had happened to Rolando, who'd seemed very much in favor earlier in the day.

"No." Jane giggled. "It's just Rolando's nickname. Only special people get to call him by it, though, like his mom—and me."

"I see." Nina exchanged covert smiles with Sophie. "I guess, if this weather keeps up, he won't be coming out to tend the garden tomorrow."

"Actually," Jane said with feigned nonchalance, "I was going to ask you about that. I mean, would it be okay if he came out anyway? Like for dinner, maybe?"

"That can probably be arranged, if Sophie doesn't mind the extra work."

Jane rushed to volunteer her services. "I'll help," she offered. "I'll make that cake, Sophie, the one I made the first day I met him. And we'll do the dishes after dinner, so you don't have to."

"You will not," Sophie announced firmly. "I, too, have to face *le papa* when he comes home. There will be no hanky-panky in my kitchen when my back is turned."

Jane blushed prettily. "He's not my boyfriend, you know. He's just...my friend. We've never even gone out on a date."

"Has he invited you?" Nina ventured to ask, suddenly unsettled at the idea of Jane dating. It revived too many unpleasant memories of her own tenuous grasp of the concept at the same age.

"No," Jane assured her. "Dito thinks it would be disrespectful, because he's a servant and here on trust."

A load rolled off Nina's mind. Rolando had vindicated her support and reinforced her good opinion of him with that statement. "He most certainly is not a servant, Jane, and I hope you told him so, otherwise he won't feel comfortable accepting a dinner invitation from you."

"I know, and I did tell him, but I think he'd feel better if he knew you wanted him to come, too. Is it okay if I phone and tell him that you gave me permission to ask him?"

"Of course." She was such a darling, trying so hard to be the ideal daughter and guest, that Nina couldn't bear to deny her such a small request. What possible harm could there be in granting it, since both she and Hugh would be there to act as chaperons?

The rain had almost stopped by the time she crossed the garden to the garage. A few stars showed through the shredded clouds on the western horizon though their light was too feeble to relieve the utter blackness of Hugh's apartment. It didn't matter. Nina was as familiar with its layout as she was with her own bedroom and scarcely needed her flashlight to make her way through the tiny entrance hall and into the large bed-sitting room.

It took only a couple of minutes to leave candles in holders by the bed and on the dresser. She noticed that the window above the easy chair was open and reached up to close it, just in case it rained heavily again, later on.

She was in the bathroom, setting candles on the vanity, when she thought she heard something. It was less a noise than a faintly audible sigh, as if the air had been disturbed by the stealthy opening of a door.

Apprehension stroked down her spine. Even though, strain her ears as she might, she couldn't detect another sound, she knew with cold certainty that she was no longer alone in the apartment. She could feel another's presence, sense the menace of someone poised to strike. And she knew, since his flight was not due for another two hours at the earliest, that, whoever it was who had followed her through the unlocked door, he was not Hugh.

There was a sense of waiting, the intruder for her to make a mistake, and she for him to trip or stumble and advertise his exact whereabouts. How loudly her heart thumped! Surely he'd hear and discover her, trapped in the small bathroom with no place to hide, except behind the shower curtain.

Oh, Lord, why had she ever watched that terrifying movie, *Psycho*?

"One of these days," Barney BMW had often predicted with ghoulish satisfaction, "you're going to regret being such a bleeding heart with these pint-size felons! One of them's going to see you for the softie you are and take you to the cleaners. I'd keep deadbolts on all my doors, if I were you."

Why hadn't she listened? And which of the dozens of teenagers she'd come into contact with over the last several months had shown any sort of violent or psychotic tendencies?

Why was she wasting time playing guessing games, when she ought to be trying to steal out of the front door?

He was expecting her. She got no more than ten feet inside the main room before he lunged, catching her off balance and sending the flashlight skittering across the floor. Before she could react, either with rage or fear, he had one of her arms in a hammerlock. Red hot needles of pain, so acute they incapacitated her, shot from her wrist to her shoulder.

His knee in the small of her back sent her flying across the bed, smothering her face down on the cotton quilt. She could hear each savage breath he drew, feeling the iron and granite that made up his frame, and knew that she could never match his strength, that the only way to escape him was to outwit him.

Effortlessly wrenching her over on to her back, he straddled her and looped his hands around her throat with all the lethal intent of a hangman's noose. Instinct brought up her knee, but he was faster and, flinging himself down on top of her, clamped her thigh with his. "Try that again, you little bastard," he assured her with absolute conviction, "and I'll kill you!"

It would never have occurred to her to doubt him, had it not been for one thing: she knew that voice, even disguised as it was with fury and a quiet sort of desperation. And, even though she'd never before felt it pinned to hers in quite such intimacy, she knew that body. Her assailant was the tallest, leanest, most attractive man she'd ever met. And at that moment, he was also the meanest.

"Hugh!" His name emerged as a winded croak, which she barely recognised and which he ignored.

"Save it!" he hissed and, just in case she felt disposed to defy him, he pressed his thumbs more cruelly against her windpipe.

The pain was excruciating. She writhed, let out a thin wail, and struck blindly at his face. The rasping of her nails over day-old beard growth shrilled in the darkness. He would bear scars, tomorrow.

He recoiled and suddenly eased the pressure on her throat as his fingertips embarked on a Braille-like examination of her face. Starting with her jaw, they traveled the length of her cheek to her eyes, fanned lightly over her lashes and smoothed her brows, then wove themselves through the loosened braid of her hair.

The tempo of his breathing altered, from rapid to erratic, and he swore, softly and emphatically, his lips so close to hers that she could almost feel the shape of each expletive as it left his tongue. His hands slid down her neck, settled again at her throat in mute apology, and continued their exploration, sweeping the length of her arms to her fingertips. Thoughtfully, he tested the length of her nails, buffed the pad of his thumb over their lacquered surface.

He found her waist, gauging its dimension with spanned hands and then, as though seeking the ultimate proof, flattened his palms against her ribs and let his thumbs trace the underside curve of her breasts.

"Nina?" he breathed, horrified.

"Who else?" she returned in a shattered whisper, melting with a pleasure more terrifying than her earlier fear. *Don't stop*! she wanted to beg.

"For God's sake!" Groaning, he kissed her throat, her inner elbows, her wrists, seeking out all the bruises he'd inflicted and trying to erase each one. Finally, his lips came to rest on hers. "What," he demanded, in between a flurry of kisses half penitent, half punitive, "were you doing, creeping around here in the dark?"

"Candles," she gasped, flames of passion licking through her. "There's a power...failure...I didn't want you..."

"Shut up," he said thickly, and kissed her again, differently this time. With scrupulous attention to detail, he memorized the shape of her mouth; sought and gained entry past her lips, tasting her heat and reveling in it.

Flames rose up inside her, taking such hold that she thought she'd suffocate. Her heart fluttered, trapped in a space too small to contain it. Never before in her life had she felt so completely, joyously alive. The tip of his tongue dallied with hers, sending a shower of delight running over her, puckering her nipples and creating total havoc with her limbs, which seemed weighted with incredible and irresistible lassitude. She clung to him, twined herself to him, begging shamelessly without saying a word.

He knew. Shifting until he was lying half across her, he scooped her against him. She knew he was going to touch her in places and ways never allowed to another man, and felt her flesh begin to tremble. All those landmarks by which she'd mapped her way through the last fifteen years blurred around the edges. For the first time, she was not haunted by shame or caution, was not afraid of the direction in which she was headed. Instead, she knew a sense of having at last come to terms with a destiny that had been inevitable from the moment she'd first set eyes on him.

This was the man who was going to set her free to live the rest of her life. She wanted him to make love to her, now, and she knew he wanted the same thing. It didn't matter that he made no promises about what came after.

It mattered only that he wanted her with the same raging honesty that she wanted him.

His knee cajoled her thighs apart, his mouth sought out her nipple through the fabric of her blouse, his hands uncovered her. Driven beyond patience to feel all of him naked against her, she attacked his clothing and heard the soft pop of buttons tearing away from his shirt.

He felt like silk, lightly sandpapered with hair. He felt like steel, tempered by the heat of inconceivable passion. Her fingernails raked lightly over him again, claws sheathed this time. She heard his breath catch sharply, then his hand came down to cover hers, detaining her, detaining both of them.

It was too late. A trembling, invisible but potent, took hold of her from the inside out, clamoring for release until she heard the silent voices screaming within her. And then they weren't silent at all. She was begging him, crying out his name over and over. "Hugh...Hugh...!" And it was a prayer, a mantra.

When he'd seen the play of the flashlight beam on his window, he'd been sure it was that Hispanic boy with his sly charm that was just a front for trouble, and a violence had risen up in him the like of which he hadn't known since he'd been released from the hell of Colombia. It could have killed her, would have killed her, if the scent of her hadn't chased away the madness, and the feel of her hadn't restored him to a shocked realization of who and where he was. But now, at the sound of her voice, it swept over him again, with altered intent.

It cared nothing for finesse or tenderness, was concerned only with its own voracious appetite. He'd thought about her for too long, wanted her too much. Try as he might, he couldn't fight this other dragon, too.

Her nipples teased his chest, her thighs hugged his hips. Savour this moment, his brain urged. Cherish her.

Take her, his body raged. Just once before you die, taste paradise!

Then she touched him, closing possessive fingers around him, and the battle was over. Primeval instinct took charge, driving him to bury himself deep inside her and brand her with the permanent mark of his possession.

Nina heard a wild and distant thunder that was her own heartbeat closing in on her, out of control, the rhythmic pulsing gone mad until one long, cataclysmic explosion shot the air from her lungs and sent her flying, weightless, to the far edge of sanity and beyond.

She thought perhaps she cried out, because he answered her in a deep, quiet voice rough textured with passion. He held her as if he'd defy God before he'd let her go, and kept her safe until the fury passed. Then, as the tumult lessened and the roaring of her blood slowed, she sank with him into a lilting half world of sighs and murmurings, and tiny tender kisses strung together with words of love that made no sense, except to the two of them.

She threaded her fingers through his hair, the way she'd always wanted to, and he turned his face toward her arm and pressed his mouth to the pulse at her wrist. "Some power failure!" he murmured, ruefully.

As if on command, there was a humming noise and the lamp by the front door came on. The dials on the stereo glowed green, followed a second later by music, something soft and sexy, designed for lovers.

"You aren't supposed to be here yet," Nina began.

Simultaneously, he said, "I'm not really a lunatic."

"I know." She reached up and smoothed the furrows from his forehead.

Abruptly, he caught at her hand and angled her wrist towards the lamplight. "Oh, good God!" His expression registered disgust at the red marks he'd left on her skin.

"I bruise easily," she said.

He rolled away from her. "That hardly makes me feel any better."

His eyes were hooded, bleak, fixed on something light years removed from her, and the distance stretched coldly between them. She shivered. "Tell me," she begged.

He knew exactly what she meant. "I guess you've got a right to know, after tonight's manic performance."

"Not if it's too painful." Most of all, she wanted to bring him back to the present, to her, but if talking could release him from whatever it was in his past that haunted him she was ready to listen all night.

"I don't know if it's painful any more, because I never let myself dwell on it." He drew in a sigh and, folding his hands behind his head, stared up to where reflections from the pool chased across the ceiling. "But it follows me everywhere I go and sneaks up on me when I'm not expecting it, and I just react. Maybe it's time I talked about it—got the whole damn business out of my system once and for all. But I should warn you, you might not feel the same about me, after."

A thought swam out of nowhere to the forefront of her mind, burning to be asked. "Is it to do with Sandra?" Nina whispered, because if it was then she wasn't sure she wanted to hear, after all. Not after he'd just made love to her. Just for tonight, he belonged to her and she wasn't willing to share him, not even with a dead woman.

He turned perceptive eyes towards her and, reaching out one hand, tucked his long, strong fingers around hers. "No, my darling, it has nothing to do with Sandra. There was no room left in my heart for her, even before I met you."

"Then tell me all of it," she said. "I want to know."

# CHAPTER NINE

"DID you know I've worked in just about every country in the world?" Hugh asked, in the sort of conversational voice he might have used to address a stranger whom he'd just met at a rather tedious social function.

He was staring at the ceiling again but she watched him, alert to his smallest change of expression. "No, but it doesn't surprise me. I know you're one of the best in your field."

An empty smile touched his lips. "That's not why I've spent so many years living in site camps at the back end of nowhere."

"Then why?" She wanted to run her finger over his mouth and coax it into happier lines but dared not. There was a touch-me-not cast to his features that forbade any hint of sympathy. "I was running away from a mess I couldn't sort out, for all that I'd earned the reputation of being able to solve just about any geotechnical problem thrown at me. My personal life——" he spat out the words as if they left a bad taste in his mouth "—was a shambles. According to Sandra, I rated a zero as a father and something even less as a husband. And since I'm not a man who takes kindly to failure, I set myself up in situations where I could shine—in places as far away from home as I could find. Now what do you think about that?"

"I think," she said neutrally, sensing that what he'd told her so far was merely the preamble to the main story, "that you did what you thought was best, given the circumstances."

He shot her a piercing, sideways glance. "Even though it meant I virtually abandoned the child you entrusted to my care when you gave her up for adoption?"

"Well..." She floundered, searching for excuses. "It was better than exposing her to constant fighting, I suppose."

"Dear Nina," he chided, "even you, a woman used to finding some good in all the sinners that cross your path, can't really condone what I did—and continued to do, even after Sandra died, for that matter. I walked away from my obligations. Ran out on my child. Left her in the neurotic care of a woman I refused to live with, because it was easier than staying and dealing with the problem."

Nina knew he was oversimplifying the situation. She remembered, even if he didn't, what he'd once told her about Sandra's possessiveness toward Jane, and of how she'd shut him out of both their lives. "What would you change, given the chance to do it all over again?"

He laughed, then, a sour, bitter sound. "Not get married!"

"And miss having Jane for a daughter?"

"She might have been better off."

"I doubt she'd agree. She adores you, Hugh."

"Why? Because twice a year I showed up and took her away from her mother for a few weeks? I hardly think so. The two of them were inseparable."

He was determined to paint the blackest picture of his omissions and failures, as though his doing so would force her to defend his actions. But someone else's forgiveness didn't mean a thing if a person couldn't forgive himself. That was a lesson she'd learned a long time ago. "Is this the reason you're so prone to attack people in the dark?" she asked lightly. "Or do you have a better reason?"

The ghost of a real smile crossed his face. "In other words, stop stalling and get on with it, right?"

"Something like that."

"Well, when word reached me that Sandra was dead, I panicked. All at once, I was sole parent and guardian of a girl who was practically a stranger and who nursed toward me a real resentment that had been carefully cultivated by her mother.

"On top of that, I knew diddly-squat about teenage girls in general. So I sent her off to boarding school, telling myself it was the best thing for both of us. It left me free to pursue my career, which meant I could provide all the material comforts to which life with Sandra had accustomed Jane, and other people, better equipped than I'd ever be, would take over the business of seeing her through her difficult teenage years. That's what I was paying hefty fees for, after all. I was royally ticked off when she got thrown out of one school after another, and I had to keep putting projects on hold to fly back home, sort out the mess, and get her settled some place else."

He shook his head. "They were some reunions, I can tell you! First, the current headmistress would make it pretty plain that my child fell conspicuously short of the standards expected of students at her school. Jane was disruptive, insolent, unruly—very undesirable qualities which could not be allowed to infect other girls. Then Jane would be brought in and promptly prove every word the woman had said was right on the mark. I'd ask her what she thought she was up to, causing trouble like this, and she'd glower and ask me why I wanted to know since I was never around and didn't really care, anyway."

Nina heaved a private sigh. Best intentions notwithstanding, he'd done all the wrong things. Jane hadn't needed expensive private schools, she'd needed her father, even if he hadn't been much of an expert at bringing up a daughter. Just knowing that he loved her would have earned him her forgiveness for any mistakes he might have made. Instead, he'd sent her away, distanced himself from her, and left her to grieve alone for the mother she'd loved and lost.

She took his hand, feeling terribly sorry for both the man and the child. "What happened next?"

"Shortly after I managed to get her into yet another school, I was sent to troubleshoot a project in Colombia, a few hundred miles up the Guaviare River, not far from the border with Venezuela." A mocking note crept into his voice. "It was the sort of challenge I loved: difficult terrain, physical danger, primitive conditions, corruption, graft—all the elements required to make me emerge a hero when I overcame them."

The derision faded, replaced by more somber undertones, and his eyes, Nina noticed, had taken on that remote look again. He withdrew his hand, isolating himself from all physical contact with her.

"And that," he said, "is where it all finally caught up with me, and I faced up to the fact that I couldn't run any further. It was also when I finally realized that you don't play fast and loose with life, because it's the only one you have and there's no going back for seconds, or having the chance to do better the next time around. I ran afoul of rebels who were doing a roaring trade smuggling weapons and drugs across the border, and, because I had connections in high places and might be useful, I was taken hostage."

Here it was at last, the catalyst that had changed his life, Nina realized, shivers chasing over her bare skin. The expression on his face was that of a man traumatized beyond human endurance. "The scar," she whispered, unbearably touched by his aloneness, "that's where it happened, isn't it?"

He closed his eyes, shutting her out. "Yes," he said, and, for the first time, opened his mind fully and let the memories take hold, instead of throwing up barriers to keep them at bay.

The sounds, the smells, the filth. The rough Spanish voices. That final day...

...He'd thought he might be dead and knew that if he was he'd been turned away from heaven. Only hell could smell so foul, only damnation involve such pain and humiliation. Had it been his to barter, he'd have traded his soul for a mouthful of water. Not the fetid, evil swill they'd flung at him there, but the sort he remembered from that other life: the clean, sweet taste of melted snow blended with rain and fermented to nectar under Canada's benign sun.

Outside the barred opening high above his head, a bird had screeched, disturbing the rats in the corner. They'd scuttled away into the shadows and left him with nothing but body lice for company.

The worst heat of the day had been past. He'd been able to tell from the narrow slant of sunlight angling across the ceiling, and had known that before long he wouldn't be able to see the filth littering the stone floor. Until then he'd endured the present the way he always did: by escaping into the future and remembering the past. So many plans, so many regrets.

If—*when*—he got home, he'd vowed to make up for his omissions, for having taken the line of least resistance. No more running away. He and Jane would build a new life. Somehow, they'd find what it was they'd lost all those years ago. There was still time start over, to get to know each other.

Then the pain had clenched at him again, so blindingly vicious that he'd doubled over and groaned before he could brace himself. Eternal seconds later, it had receded. Struggling out of the sweat-soaked mist, he'd conjured up his daughter's image, recalling the long, fine hair, the somber eyes, the unhappy mouth.

He'd refused to die. She'd already lost her mother—two mothers, really, if he counted the other one she'd never known. He'd be damned if she was going to have to do without her father, too. He was all she had left.

"On your feet, *gringo*!" A boot had thudded against his ribs. Above him, the flat black eyes of one of his tormentors had glowed with impersonal hatred. The fiend had spat in his face and lifted his foot a second time. "Rich, filthy *Americano*."

Even in hell, they didn't know the difference between Americans and Canadians. The fact had amused Hugh enough that he'd dared to laugh in his captor's face.

It had been a mistake. Because of that tiny gesture of contempt, his life had suddenly become expendable, the choice of starting over again with Jane no longer his to make. Desperation, or insanity, perhaps, had made him reckless. Better to go down fighting, he'd thought, than to submit meekly.

From somewhere, he'd found the strength to grab at the boot poised a third time at his head. Caught off balance, the guard had come crashing down on the stone floor. They had lain there together, face-to-face in the filth and slime, and Hugh had looked in the other man's eyes and read his own obituary.

It was then, with his final seconds ticking away, that he'd grasped at one last straw. Surely, when it was so close, he could fake death. His captors were peasants, crude and ignorant. They took their pleasure from inflicting punishment; there was no entertainment for them

in tormenting a body past pain. And they were super-
stitious about departed spirits. Once convinced that
they'd killed him, they'd throw him out into the jungle
and leave him to rot.

"I faked a heart attack," he told Nina. "Struggled to
my feet, rolled my eyes, clutched my chest, and fell face
first on the floor again. But before I did, I let that bastard
have it right in the face. I heard his nose crack, saw his
teeth fly out, and I knew the most animalistic satisfaction that, even now, it makes me sick to talk about
it."

He heard her indrawn breath, felt her fingers clutch
his. "But did you fool them?"

"Not entirely. Another guard bludgeoned me with his
rifle butt and split my skull for good measure, which
made it easy for me to lie there comatose in a pool of
my own blood. Just as I'd expected, they hauled me out
and left me in the jungle. Fortunately, I was past caring
about what might happen if no one rescued me before
I bled to death or the wildlife got to me."

"How did you escape?"

"With extreme difficulty. A friendly tribe found me
and took care of me until I was able to travel. Then they
drew a map, gave me a few supplies, and pointed me in
the direction of the border. I traveled at night, hid during
the day, and slept with one eye open. Once, the rebels
almost stepped on me where I lay hidden. It took me
almost a month to make it to safety and another two
before I was released from hospital and able to fly home.
And the really remarkable thing was that Jane was glad
to see me."

Nina's vision blurred. What did one say to a man
who'd been to hell and lived to tell about it? His voice,
as he'd related the sequence of events, had betrayed
scarcely a hint of emotion, yet the tension had radiated

from him like live wires. He'd given her a stripped-down account, omitting many of the details, but it didn't require much imagination to fill in the blanks. One look at him was enough. Apart from his heaving chest, he lay motionless on the bed, hands clenched by his sides, cold beads of sweat dotting his upper lip and forehead.

Sorrow welled up inside, seeping through her veins to stream into the most secret corners of her body. Sorrow, and something more that made words seem empty and barren: a deeply felt need to comfort that owed nothing to pity, nor even sympathy, but that stemmed from fear. How close she'd come to never knowing him, to never having the chance to love him! Gratitude that hinged on prayer showed her the path to take. Bending over him, she laid her lips on his. He felt cold, drained. She pressed her hands to his cheeks, gathered his mouth warmly to hers and stirred him to new life, not with the same explosion of fire that had devoured him the first time they'd made love, but with a slow igniting of the senses that healed his hurts and woke him to new beginnings.

His eyes fell shut, no longer haunted. His arms came up to bind her to him, his touch skimming over her as lightly as a spring breeze. Moved in a way she'd never expected by his gentleness, she struggled to contain a sob, but it escaped, pushed out by a dozen others.

He felt them racking her body and turned to kiss the palm of her hand. "Don't cry," he said. "You'll make me think you're sorry I survived."

"Oh, Hugh!" Her laughter was full of tears. Not from pity—he couldn't have endured that—but from sharing the pain. His heart twisted and sent a sharp little pain shooting through his chest. She was the kind of woman he'd been looking for all his life, and thought he'd never find.

They slipped into lovemaking as effortlessly as though God had fashioned them expressly for each other and this moment. No haste, no uncertainty. Their coming together was a warm and lovely celebration of everything that was good and right between a man and a woman.

Nina was all classic grace and amber silk in the soft light, her neck and arms as poetic as a ballerina's, the dark swath of her hair a curtain drawn between him and the rest of the world. Hugh wished the night need never end; wished with a futile ache that he'd been the one she'd turned to at fifteen, that he'd fathered her baby and thereby forged immutable bonds with her.

His hands slid to her hips, held her braced above him, a heartbeat short of complete unity. He touched her, probing... retreating... And when her indrawn breath told him he'd teased them both enough, he took possession of her with a smooth and ancient rhythm that acknowledged no other time or place, because only the here and now mattered.

He saw the delicate flush of pleasure that highlighted her cheeks, the soft imprint of her teeth indenting her lip, the sudden question in her eyes as control threatened to elude her, and he yearned to take her beyond anything she'd ever known or dreamed of with any other lover.

He felt the brief clenching of her flesh, the minute quivering that rolled over her as the tide of desire approached its inevitable conclusion, and knew a wild exultation. Then he stopped thinking altogether, too swept up in the wonder of having, of holding, of taking and giving generously, without question of right or reward.

His mind swirled with pinpricks of light, distancing the ordinary world to a very faraway point. Helpless, he allowed the fluid passion to soar between them, looping around them and weaving a web of incredible, unforgettable magic hemmed with tenderness.

"I think I love you," he muttered at last against her mouth, and immediately restored appalled sanity. It had been years since he'd told a woman he loved her, and even longer since he'd believed it. How had Nina managed to ambush a heart so well protected? Such an occurrence wasn't part of his blueprint, at all.

When will you be sure? she almost asked, wanting so much more than he seemed able to give. She knew that the words hadn't grown cold on his lips before he doubted them. She could feel it in the sudden slackness of his arms around her, in the way his eyes flew open and focused intently on the ceiling, avoiding all contact with hers. They were as physically close as it was possible for two people to be, yet a chill chased over her skin as though it were the middle of winter and he'd pushed her out into the cold.

His chest shuddered on a bewildered sigh. "I hadn't bargained on——"

"Hush!" She laid a finger to his lips, cherishing him with her eyes. "Don't say anything else, not yet."

"They aren't easy words," he began again, "at least, not for me, and..."

"I wouldn't want to hear them if they were, and you didn't have to say them now, just because we made love."

*Liar*! They were the *only* reason for two people to make love! They were the only words that could justify such intimacy. They were the only words that she wanted to say to him, because her heart was so full, nothing else would do.

"Nina?"

"It might be a very good idea," she said, "if I were to get dressed and go back to the house before Sophie or Jane comes to investigate the length of time it's taking me to leave a couple of candles in your room."

"God forbid!" Laughter softened his reply, but his eyes remained serious and he did nothing to try to dissuade her.

She untangled herself from him and reached for her clothes. "Shall I tell Jane you're home already?"

"No. It's getting late." He touched her back, running his hand lightly down her spine. "Assuming that all's well with her, it can wait until tomorrow."

He walked with her to the door, dropped a last kiss on her mouth, smiled at her. He waited until she'd crossed the garden and climbed the steps to the main house before he closed his door, all of which ought to have made her feel protected, cherished. Yet a distance lingered about him, leaving her feeling as if he'd rung down the final curtain and planned no encores.

Don't be greedy! she scolded herself. Maybe he just needed time to get used to the idea of falling in love. That was certainly something she could understand because, although she'd known from the very beginning that she was attracted to him, not until tonight had she fully acknowledged that her feelings ran much deeper, and the shock was only now beginning to recede.

But instinct told her it wasn't that simple. As surely as if he'd admitted it himself, she knew that he would have unsaid those words if he could, and she was dismayed at how bereft that made her feel.

"Daddy!" Jane was ecstatic to see him the next morning, and flew across the terrace to meet him as he came up to the house for breakfast.

The smile that lit his face at the sound of her voice faded into annoyance at the sight of her. "What in the world happened to your hair?"

She skidded to a halt, muttering, "I got it cut, that's all," and tugged wisps of it forward to cover up her ears.

Nina, seeing the pleasure on Jane's face melt into a scowl that matched Hugh's, had the premonition that all her pessimistic fears were about to be compounded. There was no remnant of last night's lover in the man confronting her now, nor of the fond father as he inspected Jane. Nina wondered if he had any idea how daunting his greeting was to a girl whose self-confidence had already taken more of a beating than most.

"It was my idea, Hugh," she said calmly, feeling obliged to shoulder the lion's share of the blame. "Her hair badly needed trimming."

"I don't call that trimming," he retorted, observing his daughter closely. "I call that being shorn."

"Well, I like it," Jane informed him defiantly. "It makes me look more sophisticated."

"Sophisticated, my foot! And if you like it so much, why are you hanging on to your ears as if you're afraid they'll catch cold?"

"Hugh," Nina began again, but Jane cut her off.

"I like these, too!" she announced and, lowering her hands, swung her head back and forth, flaunting her gold sleepers.

For a moment, Hugh didn't speak. He seemed to have trouble even breathing. "I cannot believe what I'm seeing," he finally declared in an ominously quiet voice.

Jane tittered, bolstered by false bravado. "Pierced ears, Dad. I always wanted them."

He flung Nina a glance so loaded with disgust that she was once again hard-pressed to believe he was the same man who, last night, had entertained even briefly the notion that he loved her.

"I suppose you're going to try to justify this by telling me that her ears needed trimming, too?" he snapped, and, without waiting to hear what, if any, reply she had to offer, swung back to Jane. "And you're too young to know what you want. In fact, you change your mind so often that I doubt you can remember today what it was you thought you couldn't live without yesterday."

"I do so!"

He paid not the slightest attention, but continued with chilling disapproval, "Furthermore, you took advantage of my absence to do something to which you knew full well I would object. I'm very disappointed in you, Jane. You promised me, the day I agreed not to send you back to boarding school, that there'd be no more of this sort of sneaky behavior."

"You should talk!" she shot back, stung. "You promised me that we'd have the whole summer together, and already you're flying off and leaving me, just like you did before."

"It couldn't be helped. It was only for a few days, and I left you with Nina which, at the time, seemed a good idea." He rolled his eyes, as though to say that he must have been mad to leave such a witless creature in charge of a minor.

"Right," Jane declared with all the blithe cruelty of youth. "So who needs to have you show up now and spoil things?"

Nina's heart bled for him. He blinked and said gently, "I'm still your father, Jane."

"Nina's my mother, and I got along fine with just one parent before, so what's the big deal now?"

"Jane!" Nina stretched out a restraining hand, but Hugh stopped her with a glare.

"No," he insisted, "let her finish. There's nothing my daughter can't say to me. Our bonds are not that easily severed. Finish what you started, Jane."

Jane looked discomfited, suddenly uncertain of her role. The little girl in her, Nina guessed, longed to rush into her father's arms and say she was sorry; the young woman, however, held back, too proud to admit to such weakness.

Sadly for everyone, pride won. "Well, isn't that what you said you wanted? For me to get to know my real mother? Well, I have, and I like it. *Nina* understands I'm not a child any more. She said it was okay for me to get my ears pierced—and for me to date Rolando. He's coming for dinner, tonight, so there!"

Hugh blanched with rage. "*What*?"

He covered the few yards that separated him from Nina, came to a stop so close that she had to tilt up her head to look him in the eye, and without so much as a by-your-leave dragged her far enough away from Jane that he could speak his mind without being overheard.

"Did you think," he inquired in a near whisper, practically backing Nina into a lilac bush, "that because you extended sexual favors to me last night I would feel obliged to let you get away with murder this morning?"

She tried to contain her dismay because she knew he'd notice and correctly infer that she was devastated. "That would be funny," she retorted with admirable calm, "if it weren't so incredibly insulting."

"Funny?" he snapped. "Why aren't I laughing, then? I'll tell you why, Miss Interfering Sommers—because this is just another pathetic example of your manipulative efforts to buy other people's approval without any regard for the consequences. Well, this time you miscalculated. I am *not* going to stand idly by and play the heavy to your Lady Bountiful. If I have to shoulder all the blame for the problems arising in Jane's life—and it's been my experience that I do—then I intend to exercise full control in trying to prevent them. I am in charge of Jane, now, not you or anyone else.''

Nina stood her ground. ''Did it ever occur to you, Hugh, that I have some rights, too?''

''You have no rights where my daughter is concerned!''

''I'm her natural mother.''

''You're a bloody *un*natural mother if you gave permission for her to get her body carved up.'' His mouth twisted in disgust. ''But then, why should I have expected anything different from a woman who finds it perfectly acceptable to expose a girl of fifteen to an excon? Come to think of it, she's got a lot more in common with him now, with those bloody stupid rings in her ears, hasn't she? Maybe he'll even see fit to visit a barber and get his damned ponytail chopped off, then they can pretend they're twins!''

She wanted to tell him that he was getting himself all worked up over nothing. That if Jane decided she didn't want holes in her ears they'd close up once she stopped wearing pierced earrings; that the last thing she wanted was to usurp his role in Jane's life; that she thought he was a wonderful father, most of the time, and much too fair to judge a young man on the strength of his appearance.

But, ''You're a bloody unnatural mother'', he'd said, and it didn't matter that Jane had called her ''Mom''— surely the best indication yet that her daughter's early resentment toward her had given way to a growing fondness—because, with a certainty that had been conspicuously absent from last night's declaration of love, Hugh had just negated her as being of any real consequence in Jane's life.

She opened her mouth to refute him but the hurt swelled up, blocking the way, and she burst into tears, something she hadn't done for more years than she cared to remember.

"Oh, good God!" Hugh flung up his hands in fury. "Stop it! If you think that's going to soften me up, you're wrong. I grew immune to crying jags years ago, and I'm frankly surprised you'd resort to yet another clichéd attempt to undermine my judgment. Stop it, I said!"

He was unjust. He was insensitive. He was unkind. And he had the capability to hurt her beyond anyone else she'd ever known. "Don't flatter yourself!" she wailed, just enough anger creeping back to allow her to enunciate. She hated having him witness such an abject display of weakness, and hated even more the implication that she'd barter her body in exchange for maternal privileges. "Do you think I like standing here with my nose running, while you watch? It's almost as embarrassing as knowing that, last night, I——"

"We're not alone," he reminded her curtly. "Be careful what you say!"

She pushed the tears away from her face with the heel of her hand. "Oh, don't worry, Hugh. I won't say anything that might sully your image in front of Jane. You're doing a good enough job of that all by yourself, without any help from me."

"Then it can't hurt further when I tell you that in no circumstances will I allow Rolando Torres to have dinner with my daughter tonight."

Jane, drawn toward them by the sight of Nina mopping at her tears, heard and let out a wail of distress. "Daddy, you have to! Please! If you don't, I'll—I'll run away!"

# CHAPTER TEN

"No." HUGH stood there, arms crossed, feet planted apart, as arrogant as the King of Siam. "And don't you dare to try to blackmail me with threats, young lady, because I won't put up with it."

"Need I remind you," Nina cut in, "that this is my house and I can invite whom I please to be my guest here?"

"And must I so soon again remind you," Hugh countered implacably, "that Jane is my daughter and will do as I say? We will dine out tonight and be back late, so please don't wait up for us."

"I hate you!" Jane cried, her face crumpling.

"I'll survive," Hugh replied stoically. "You're not the first to feel that way about me, and you obviously aren't the last."

But his eyes, Nina noticed, as they flickered briefly toward hers, looked bleak and for all his mammoth self-control he couldn't quite disguise the hurt.

Jane loves you, she wanted to tell him, and so, God help me, do I. Please don't treat us as if we're the enemy. This is something we can work out.

But she knew he'd rebuff her. He was in no mood to be swayed by reason or tenderness, and refused to be moved despite Jane's tearful pleas and apologies. If, as so many experts maintained, the key to successful parenting lay in firm and consistent discipline, Hugh would have graduated at the top of the class.

Early in the afternoon, he bundled Jane in his car and drove off, leaving Nina with the choice either of entertaining Rolando by herself, or of phoning him with some plausible reason for canceling the date. She chose the latter, her reluctance at having to lie made that much worse by the thoughtful silence that greeted the deception, before Rolando replied, with exquisite, gentle courtesy, "I understand perfectly, *señora*. You wish me still to work as your gardener?"

Nina felt like a worm and cursed herself for allowing Hugh's pigheaded inflexibility to coerce her into taking such distasteful action. His assumption that the slightest blot on other people's copybooks precluded the possibility of their ever mending their ways was both absurd and unfair. Perhaps two and two always equaled four in the almighty world of engineering, but a man of his supposed intelligence ought to be smart enough to realize that the same unalterable logic seldom applied to the vast intangibles of human behavior.

She sighed, exasperated. By now, *she* ought to know that intellect had very little to do with objective insight where human emotions were concerned. Heaven knew, she'd dealt with enough distraught parents over the years to have learned that much, at least.

Sunday morning was horrible. The tail end of Friday's storm brought the odd shower and enough cloud to keep everyone indoors. Hugh chose to isolate himself in his own suite, ostensibly to look through the notes from his trip and prepare a report for his clients. Jane drifted about the house, alternately bored, sulky, or just plain miserable. The honeymoon, Nina thought wryly, looking at the glum faces that eventually gathered around the table for lunch, was definitely over.

Feeling she had nothing to lose, she attempted to lighten the atmosphere. "Why don't we drive into the city this afternoon? You've not seen the aquarium, Jane, have you?"

"Yes," Jane replied, flinging a sour glare at her father. "I hated it. Whales shouldn't be kept in captivity. That's something reserved for kids like me."

Hugh's pained expression warned Nina that another outbreak of hostilities was about to erupt unless she came up with a fresh diversion. "Queen Elizabeth Park, then? They have a huge, glass-domed greenhouse there that's split into climate-controlled areas to simulate different parts of the world. You can walk from desert to jungle without leaving the building."

Jane stared stolidly at her plate, clearly less than thrilled with the idea, leaving Nina to prattle on with determined good cheer, "It might give you some idea of the sort of places your father's seen in his travels."

Hugh looked up. "I'd like that," he said, unexpectedly. "Come on, Janie, take the scowl off your face and let's all call a truce. There's not that much of the summer left, so we might as well make the most of it."

Jane heaved a long-suffering sigh. "If I have to."

"And after, I'll take you on a car tour of the city," Nina cajoled, "then, if you like, we can end up for dinner in Gastown."

Hugh drummed imperious fingers on the table. "Well, Jane?"

Forced to respond, Jane offered an indifferent shrug. "If you say so."

It was not an afternoon memorable for special moments. Hugh was pleasant but reserved, and extremely careful to avoid any sort of physical contact with Nina. Jane's participation in the outing was at best dutiful and more often sullen. A wise woman, Nina well knew, would settle for mediocrity and stop mourning the absence of perfection, grateful that at least they weren't all at each other's throats. But she'd had a glimpse of paradise, and found purgatory a poor substitute.

Furthermore, as she discovered the next day, just because things appeared to have calmed down on the surface didn't mean that there weren't still undercurrents of mischief at work below, hurtling everyone toward fresh calamity. When, as forecast, Monday dawned wet and blustery, she followed through on an earlier decision to spend the morning at her office, catching up on her correspondence and dictating a few notes for Hilary. But, arriving home shortly after noon, she found Hugh waiting for her and one look at his face told her that their truce, such as it had been, was at an end.

"Where is she?" he demanded, confronting her as she came out of the garage and through the gate into the garden.

She shook open her umbrella, took a firmer grasp of her briefcase, and steeled herself to forbearance. "We're talking about Jane, I presume?"

"Naturally."

"I have no idea, Hugh. Have you checked with Sophie?"

"Yes, I've checked with Sophie, Nina. I'm not a complete idiot."

Jane's voice impinged on her memory. "I'll run away..."

"What a relief!" she replied dryly, trying to offset the apprehension fluttering in her stomach. "When did you realize Jane was missing?"

"About twenty minutes ago, after I got back from my meeting. When I spoke to her at breakfast, she didn't say anything about going out, and Sophie claims not to have seen her since just before you left for work." Suddenly, he ducked under the umbrella, stooping down to scan Nina's expression as though hoping to extract a truth she might feel disposed to hide. At the same time, his other hand grasped her upper arm. "Are you sure you don't know where she is?"

The scent of warm, damp earth and flowers enveloped them. Raindrops beat a tattoo on the silk dome of the umbrella, effectively shutting out the rest of the world. Given different, happier circumstances, he might have kissed her, and if he had, she knew he would have tasted of summer and tenderness. It would have been one of those rare moments when nature and man were in complete harmony. But too much conflict interfered, making the hand that detained her peremptory, and the eyes that searched her face untrusting.

"Quite sure," Nina stated, staring pointedly at his fingers on her arm, "so please stop acting as if you think I might have abducted her. Did you check the beach? She might have gone for a walk, even though it's so wet out."

He shook his head and briefly allowed the fear to show. "There's no sign of her."

Sophie, her face creased with dismay, waited at the back door. "Madame Nina," she began, the minute they were within earshot, "I thought for sure the child was with you or *monsieur*, otherwise I would have called at once to let you know."

So, Jane had about a three-hour start in which to put into operation a plan for revenge which, with the wisdom of hindsight, Nina realized had probably been incubating since Saturday morning. The apprehension tightened to form a cold knot of fear in the pit of her stomach. Pray heaven the girl's mischief hadn't led her into danger!

Behind her, Hugh cursed audibly. "Swearing won't help," she flung at him, "but checking her room might."

"I already did," he snapped back. "She isn't there."

"But are any of her things missing?"

He looked a little embarrassed. "I didn't take the time to look."

As far as they could determine, the room seemed almost exactly as Jane usually left it, strewn with clothes and books. By her bed was the framed photograph of Hugh and Sandra that was quite possibly her most prized possession. The only thing of any significance that was gone was her straw tote bag.

Hugh let out a sigh of obvious relief. "Well, she won't get far with a hairbrush and mirror, a keychain, half a dozen packages of gum and loose change."

It seemed to be as close as he could come to acknowledging that Jane was entirely stubborn enough to carry out her wild threat to run away. Noticing the grooves scoring his cheeks, Nina forbore to voice the frightening possibilities being played out in her overactive mind: a young girl like Jane, angry with her parents, last seen entering a stranger's car…. "Sophie," she said, steering her thoughts into more constructive channels, "exactly when was the last time you saw her?"

"Why, right before you drove away, *madame*. I heard the car and a moment later, *la petite* raced across the garden and through the side door next to the garage. Then, almost at once, the car started again, and you left."

Nina's mouth ran dry. "I parked outside the front door when we got home last night. It was more convenient, because I had a number of files to take to work this morning, and also a pile of clothing to drop off at the dry cleaner's. It couldn't have been my car you heard, Sophie."

"Well, it was not yours, *monsieur*," Sophie declared, addressing Hugh. "You did not leave for another half hour. I know because I saw you go and I remember exactly when because, only seconds before, I had looked at the clock and noticed that for the first time Rolando was late for work.''

Nina chewed her lip meditatively. "Maybe he talked to her and knows where she went.''

"I'm sure not, *madame*. He did not come at all today. I thought that perhaps, because of the rain, you had told him to stay at home.''

"No," Nina said miserably, as the one faint hope she'd managed to fan into life sank into oblivion. "As a matter of fact, when I spoke to him on Saturday, we agreed that if the ground was too wet for gardening he'd clean out the potting shed instead.''

She heard Hugh inhale sharply and knew that even before she'd finished speaking he'd added two and two and come up with another perfect four. "My daughter disappeared just about the time Rolando Torres was supposed to show up and didn't, and you heard an engine outside the garage, which is where he always parks that infernal machine?" he barked at Sophie and, when she nodded mute agreement, snatched up the phone.

"Well, counselor," he said with quiet fury, jabbing a finger at the call buttons, "I hope you're satisfied! Is there any doubt in your mind about where we should start looking for Jane?''

"There certainly is," Nina retorted, reading his mind only too clearly. "The fact that Jane is missing is not Rolando's fault, so if you're phoning the Torres's household, I suggest you refrain from making unfounded accusations otherwise you might find yourself facing me in a court of law, because I definitely will not allow you to harass that family without due cause.''

"Save the threats," he shot back scornfully. "I have no intention of communicating with the Torres family. This is something the police can handle. They should have been called hours ago.''

"You might very well be right. Just don't bring Rolando's name into it."

Hugh held the phone away from his ear long enough to fling her an incredulous stare. "Forget it, Nina. What you do to protect your little gang of hoodlums is your own business—until my child gets drawn in, and then it becomes mine. If you think I'm about to pussyfoot around, playing Mr. Nice Guy, while Rolando Torres is out there somewhere with Jane, think again!"

Before she could reply, he spoke into the phone, spitting out his name, address and phone number, and concluding with, "I want to file a report. My daughter is missing."

"Hugh, please!" Nina implored.

He turned his back on her. "Almost sixteen...since about nine this morning... What do you mean, wait twenty-four hours? I don't care what the regular policy is, this is not a regular case. My daughter is a stranger in this city and I have every reason to believe she's in the company of a known criminal element."

"If it turns out that you're wrong, I'll never forgive you for this," Nina promised him as he hung up the phone.

"That makes two of us, then, because I'll never forgive you. You've known all along how I feel about exposing Jane to that boy's influence, yet you've gone ahead and done things your way without any regard for my opinions." He made a slashing motion with one hand as though, if he could, he'd wipe her off the face of the earth. "Your problem is that you're so consumed with guilt because you got pregnant and gave up your baby for adoption that you keep trying to atone with every other kid you come across, even now that you've found Jane and ought to be making her your first consideration."

"Just as she's always been yours, you mean?"

She'd scored with that reply. She could tell by the way he drew himself up to his full height, his back soldier-straight.

"Oh, brother!" He pursed his lips in a silent whistle. "For someone who prides herself on being compassionate, you surely know how to go for the jugular."

He felt betrayed by her. This whole mess had arisen because she insisted on allowing her professional associations to intrude on her private life. The bottom line, as he saw it, was that she was prepared to put Rolando Torres first. Ahead of Jane. Ahead of him—even as she cast her net at him so temptingly that he'd entertained the idea that she was one woman he could trust enough to love!

Well, they did say, didn't they, that there was no fool like an old fool? What would it take for him to come to terms with what he'd suspected from the outset: that he was merely the means to an end? It wasn't the newfound man she wanted, it was her long-lost child—but not if it meant forsaking her Pollyanna theories about reformed youth. He might not always be the wisest father, or the most diplomatic, but at least he loved Jane enough to put her interests ahead of some streetwise delinquent's.

Bitterly, he stared out at the gray afternoon. To think he'd been on the verge of entering into a business partnership that would have found him settling permanently on the West Coast, within easy miles of Nina—and all because he'd thought she'd be good for Jane, and perhaps even for him!

Well, that was one mistake it wasn't too late to rectify. As soon as Jane was back safe where she belonged, in his custody, they'd be hightailing it back home, and if Nina's maternal instincts were really as intense as she proclaimed them to be she could be the one to do the visiting in future.

As for himself, if he craved female diversion once in a while, that was easily fixed, too. There were plenty of women who'd be happy to accommodate him for the price of a night on the town, without cutting his heart out in the process. God knew, he didn't need another failed relationship on his conscience. One was enough!

The front doorbell chimed. "That'll be the police," he said. "I'll let them in."

Her dark, beautiful eyes beseeched him. "Please, Hugh——"

"Save it," he said curtly, and strode out of the room.

They gathered around the table in the dining room. The officers were sympathetic. "I understand your concern," the older of the pair said, after he'd taken down the particulars. "I've got a couple of teenagers myself—that's why I'm gray before my time—but let's not go assuming the worst. Now, about this Torres boy, what can you tell us that might help us locate him?"

"He's been in trouble with the law before, more than once," Hugh told them. "He lives with his family above the Hacienda Restaurant in Bootleg Alley, but I doubt you're going to find him there."

"We'll check the place out. Meantime, what about a car, or a license plate number?"

"He runs around on an old motorbike." Hugh indicated Nina with a toss of his head. "Ask her," he said bitterly. "She probably knows, but you won't get her to admit it voluntarily."

"Miss Sommers?"

Nina shook her head. "All I can tell you is that he owns a restored Norton—and that I don't think Rolando is in any way responsible for my daughter's disappearance."

The officer exchanged puzzled glances with his junior partner and directed his next question at Hugh. "Isn't the missing girl your daughter, sir?"

"She's mine, too," Nina informed him, anxiety and rage leaving her dangerously close to tears. "And I'm as worried as her father. I just don't happen to believe in trying to incriminate someone else in her disappearance until there's reason to suppose he's guilty."

"Has your daughter ever threatened to run away? Because of trouble within the family, say?" The gray-haired man regarded them both shrewdly. "A disagreement of some sort, perhaps?"

"Yes." Nina blinked furiously, and glared at Hugh. "She was upset because her father wouldn't let her associate with Rolando. We had quite an argument about it on Saturday."

"The kid's a delinquent!" Hugh roared. "What sort of father would I be to agree to her hanging around with someone like that?"

Everyone began talking at once then, the police trying to restore order, Sophie calling on higher powers to intervene, Nina and Hugh snarling and snapping like angry dogs fighting over a bone. Yet above all the noise, they somehow sensed the presence of new arrivals and turned as one toward the couple standing in the doorway.

Jane's clear voice cut through the bedlam as incisively as a knife through butter. "Why is everyone yelling?"

The silence was brief but deafening. Nina thought she'd never forget the successive expressions that flitted over Hugh's face: anxiety erased by relief which, in turn, was chased away by black anger as his gaze shifted from Jane to Rolando who stood beside her.

"Easy, sir!" The younger police officer, sizing up the situation, intervened as Hugh lunged to his feet. "Let us handle this."

Nina sprang up, too, relief churning through her in great, rolling waves. For the first time, she allowed herself to admit how deathly afraid she'd felt because of Jane's disappearance. She knew better than most how easy it was for a person to drop off the edge of the world without leaving a trace. She'd done it herself, when she was just about Jane's age. She'd moved across the country and never gone home again. By the time she'd been ready to make peace with her mother, the poor woman had been dead. "Oh, sweetheart," she whispered, hugging Jane fiercely, "I'm so glad to see you! We've been worried sick."

"I'm sorry," Jane mumbled, hiding her face in Nina's neck. "I was just so mad, you know?" Then she stiffened in the embrace and pushed away, seeming to notice the uniforms for the first time. "Who called the police?"

"I did," Hugh said through clenched teeth, restraining himself with an obvious effort.

"Why, Daddy?"

"Because I suspected that Rolando Torres was responsible for your disappearance and I was obviously right."

"Oh!" Jane's face flushed scarlet with mortification. "Daddy, how could you do this to me?"

"Jane," Hugh said with ominous patience, "the question surely is, how could you do this to us? You know how I feel about your association with this boy, yet you deliberately allowed him to coerce you into taking off without a word to anyone. I should have him arrested for kidnapping!"

"You do," Jane declared, her voice shaking with anger and imminent tears, "and I'll take off again, and this time I won't have Rolando around to talk me into coming back!"

Nina couldn't stand to keep silent a minute longer. "No one will be taking off, and no one will be arrested," she said sharply, "because no crime has been committed, so can we please put an end to all these unnecessary threats?" Politely inclining her head at the police officers, she escorted them out of the room. "I think we've taken up enough of your time, gentlemen. Thank you for coming."

She'd barely closed the front door behind them before Hugh's raised voice floated through from the dining room. Squaring her shoulders, she marched back into the fray. "All right, Hugh, that's enough!"

"Stay out of this," he warned. "It's none of your business."

"Well, I'm making it my business," she advised him. "Rolando, I don't know how you got involved in all this, or what you said or did to convince Jane to come back, but I thank you from the bottom of my heart for bringing her safely home. Jane, you and your father need to talk but not until you've both calmed down. Sophie, please take these two young people into the kitchen and give them something to eat."

She waited until they were alone before turning to Hugh. "As for you and I, we are going to set a few things straight, right now."

"I am not some teenage rebel who needs firm handling," Hugh informed her savagely.

"No, you're a grown man acting like a damn fool," she said, pouring two snifters of brandy from a decanter on the buffet and handing one to him. "Sit down with this and let us try to remember, while we decide where to go from here, that we're two supposedly reasonable adults."

They'd said cruel, unforgivable things to each other at a time when they should have been allies. Now the crisis was past and they were faced with trying to repair what they'd done to each other. But looking at the grim line of Hugh's mouth, the arctic gleam in his eyes, Nina wondered if such a thing was possible.

He poured half his drink down his throat in one swallow, then placed his glass on the table with an antagonistic thud. "If by 'we' you mean you and I, there's nothing to discuss. We've reached the end of the road. Whatever hopes I had—and I'm not too proud to admit there were a few, not all of them to do with Jane—have been effectively laid to rest by your reactions today."

Her heart started acting strangely, fluttering and stalling with dread. "Look, we were both upset and said things——"

"We're out of sync, Nina, and probably always will be," he said quietly. "That being so, Jane and I will be leaving here just as soon as I can tie up loose ends. We don't belong in your world, and you most assuredly do not belong in ours."

His words were civilized, polite, and utterly final.

"That's only your opinion."

"True," he agreed, in the same unemotional tone, "but that's the one that counts in this instance."

"You have no right to deny me access to Jane," she cried.

"Of course I haven't, nor do I propose to try. We'll work out suitable times for you to visit her."

"What if that's not enough?"

"For her," he inquired, "or for you?"

For me, in more ways than you can begin to guess! A long, slow mourning invaded her. "For her. She needs a woman in her life." Damn! Her eyes were filmed with tears and no amount of self-discipline could control the quiver in her voice. "She needs her mother, Hugh."

"Yes, in some respects she does, and there might come a time when she elects to spend most of her time with you. Until then, however..." he leveled an unyielding gaze at her "...she will live under my jurisdiction and if you want to change that you'll have to apply to the courts. I am sure I don't need to tell you, counselor, how very traumatic that can be for the children who get caught in the middle of such unpleasantness."

There was a timid tap at the door. "It's the telephone for you, *monsieur*," Sophie informed Hugh on a note of apology. "I am sorry to interrupt, but it's long distance and the caller is most insistent that he speak to you in person."

"That's all right, Sophie," Hugh said pleasantly, draining his glass. "*Madame* and I are completely finished."

# CHAPTER ELEVEN

FOR the next two days, Hugh arranged his life in such a way that he might as well have moved into a hotel for all Nina saw of him, and whatever small hope she'd nursed that they could somehow reconcile their differences withered. The night he'd told her he thought he loved her might never have happened.

As if that weren't punishment enough, though, he removed Jane from her company also. In forty-eight hours, father and daughter saw less of their hostess and more of the West Coast than they'd previously experienced in nearly six weeks.

On the third day, Nina took charge of her life again. Refusing to hang around awaiting favors obviously not forthcoming, she buried herself in her work, driving early into town and arriving home late. The day after that, just before three in the afternoon, Hilary buzzed her on the office intercom and told her she had a visitor.

It was Hugh. Surprise and shock had Nina wiping clammy hands on her tailored skirt, and hiding behind her horn-rimmed glasses.

"Sorry to interrupt you when you're busy," he began, dropping into the chair she indicated on the opposite side of her desk and leaning his head wearily on one hand, "but since we're doing such a good job of avoiding each other at the house I had no other choice. And in any case, it's probably better to discuss things here."

He looked exhausted and she couldn't quite repress the wild hope that it was the rift between them that was responsible. He soon disabused her of any such notion.

"Jane and I have had a major fight," he said. "I was awake half the night trying to figure out what's best for her."

"What caused the argument this time?"

He scowled and focused his gaze on her face as if seeking unwelcome solutions there. "Me—my work."

How he hated not being in control of the circumstances affecting his life! She could see it in every inch of him, from the tension that wired his shoulders to the uncompromising thrust of his jaw. Wisely, she refrained from saying so and asked instead, "Why are you telling me this, Hugh?"

He lunged to his feet and went to stare out of the window at the city street, sixteen floors below. "How much does Jane mean to you?" he inquired brusquely.

"I love her. You know I do."

"Yes." He sighed heavily and hunched his shoulders. "You get some harebrained notions in your head at times, but I do believe you love her and..." Another sigh, impatient this time. "Hell, I know I overreacted the other day. The Torres boy—he's not such a bad kid."

Nina knew she ought to refrain from comment, but couldn't. "Do you remember, the first day you brought Jane out to the house, asking me why I never called her by her name?"

"Yes." Somewhat puzzled, he half turned to face her. "I remember thinking it made her seem so anonymous, being referred to as 'she' and 'her' all the time, as if you were somehow denying her."

"Well, calling Rolando 'the Torres boy' does much the same thing. It robs him of the respect he deserves."

Hugh glowered. "I'm bleeding enough, Nina, without your rubbing salt in the wounds."

She adjusted her glasses and said nothing.

For twenty, perhaps thirty seconds, he struggled with hidden demons she couldn't begin to identify. When he finally spoke, it was as if the words were being torn out of him a syllable at a time. "Jane wants to live with you."

It was less an admission than a challenge, and it floored her. "What do you mean?"

"*Not* live with me."

"That's how she feels today but, as you said yourself, she changes her mind so fast that by tomorrow she'll have forgotten why she's so angry with you."

"Possibly, but that doesn't alter the fact that her basic reasoning was sound. She'll be happier with you. If I didn't truly believe that, nothing would persuade me to leave her in your custody."

Nina rearranged her hands, folding them before her on the desk. "This comes as quite a surprise, Hugh."

"What's the matter, don't you want her?"

"Yes." At last, a simple question requiring only a simple answer!

His shoulders squared briefly, then slumped, a gesture that blended defeat and relief into something so sad that it was all she could do not to rush across the room and put her arms around him. "Then you've got her," he said.

"I have a right to know why."

He prowled the room, picking up a sterling-silver letter opener, a crystal paperweight that trapped tiny rainbows within its prisms, and finally stopped before a framed eighteen-by-twenty-four blow-up of a West Coast sunset.

"I'm not going through all the details again. Once was enough, thank you. Let's just say that in my eagerness to make up for lost time I've apparently overdone the zealous father act. To put it succinctly, I'm an overbearing, judgmental oaf, and she's happier away from me. You, on the other hand, score high marks for your tolerance and understanding. Not once have you made critical reference to Sandra, no matter how great the provocation, whereas I..." His smile was bitter with self-disgust. "I am guilty, albeit with good reason, of covert maternal sabotage every time I open my mouth."

Nina could see what it cost him to admit failure so frankly. He hated what he perceived to be the only course of action left to him, just as she hated playing devil's advocate by offering yet another alternative she didn't want him to choose. "What about a fresh start for Jane at another boarding school?"

He grimaced. "I'm afraid."

"Of how she might react?"

He nodded. "She's past the age where I can bend her to my will with impunity. Damn it, a father shouldn't be afraid of his own child, but when she went missing last Saturday I felt a fear that made the whole business in Colombia seem like a village picnic, and I can't get rid of the taste of it."

"Yet you're willing to walk out of her life, again. History really does have a habit of repeating itself, doesn't it?"

He swore, savagely. "You really mean to collect your pound of flesh, don't you? You know bloody well I have no choice. I'm her father and I love her, enough to do what's best for her. Right now, with her being the age she is, she needs you. Her mother. There, I've admitted it! You were right all along. Are you satisfied?"

Nina couldn't stand his pain. It coiled between them, wrenching them both. "No," she cried, springing up and coming around the desk to grab at his hands. "No, I'm not! It shouldn't be like this. She deserves to have both parents, not just one or the other."

And it could be like that, if only he'd meet her halfway. They could all come out winners. But his face was cold and withdrawn, prohibiting overtures, and Nina would not beg. Never again would she ask a man for something he couldn't give willingly.

She squeezed her eyes shut against the memories that took her by surprise: of the night her ex-fiancé had told her that he didn't think he could marry her, after all, because of her past. Lord, how close she'd come to losing her self-respect a second time, with her coaxing and groveling!

Oh, no, never again would she beg, no matter how badly she wanted! One heart at risk was never enough. It took both parties to say "I love you," and to believe the words without doubt or reservation, if a relationship was to survive.

"Having both parents is not an option in this instance," Hugh said flatly, "and since that makes me more or less redundant, again, I've accepted another overseas assignment. A return engagement, actually."

Nina knew a sense of horror that swept aside every other concern as the implication in his words sank home. "You're not going back to Colombia? Hugh, you can't!"

"There's no personal danger involved. The area is well policed now, and, in any case, I have a professional obligation to fulfil. I'm the one they hired to deal with all the geotechnical problems, some of which still remain unresolved."

"What about your obligations to Jane?"

"Doing what's best for her means knowing when to let go." He shrugged ruefully. "Everyone will benefit if I stick to what I'm most skilled at, and leave you to do so well what you apparently come by naturally, namely understanding the teenage psyche."

"She'll miss you." *I'll* miss you.

"I'm not talking about abandoning her for months at a time. I'll be back in Canada for Christmas. As for future projects, I'll arrange my schedule around the school term so that she can spend every vacation with me. You won't deny me that, I'm sure."

"Spend those times here, at my house." She was close to begging, after all, but she didn't care. He was offering her everything she'd once thought she wanted, and now that she had it it wasn't enough. She clung to his hands, wrapping her fingers tightly around his. "Please, Hugh, don't walk out of my life like this."

He had to get away from her before she seduced him with her bribery. He untangled his hands and held her off. "That wouldn't be the smart route to take, Nina."

"Why not? Why won't you take a chance on us as a threesome?"

Those silly glasses slid to half-mast down her elegant nose, magnifying her already dense lower lashes. He didn't want to look at her lovely face, and he didn't want to listen to the low, sweet melody of her voice, luring him into decisions that he'd live to regret.

Gently, he extended a finger and poked the glasses back on to that narrow, aristocratic bridge. "You really ought to get a prescription pair," he murmured hoarsely. "These drugstore numbers aren't good for you. They don't fit properly."

"What is good for me?" she asked, and he thought he'd drown in the limpid depths of her beautiful eyes.

"Not me," he said with a fine disregard for grammar, and stepped out of touching range. The temptations were just too great. If he'd thought himself capable of kissing her just once and then stopping, he'd have indulged himself one last time. But he didn't dare.

"Not very long ago, you told me you thought you loved me," she said, her voice quavering like a child's, "and I wanted so much to believe it."

"I never should have said that," he muttered. "I've been alone so long, I don't know how to share myself any more. I'll hurt you and disappoint you, and eventually all the good things we might share will turn sour and you'll resent me. I'm too old to go through that sort of grief again."

Her eyes filled and he turned away, feeling as if his heart was being torn loose and tossed about at the whim of her unhappiness. Damn, oh, damn!

"I'm not Sandra," she said. "I'm not out to take everything you've got to give without offering something in return. I love you. I think I've loved you from the moment I first saw you."

"Stop it!" he raged. "I don't want your love!"

His heart was laying traps, giving him one more reason not to do what cool, objective intellect had convinced him was the best thing for everyone concerned. He didn't think he was an evil man, and he got no pleasure from deliberately trying to hurt other people. Yet, through neglect or insensitivity or just sheer incompetence, he'd alienated first a wife and then a daughter. There came a time when a man had to stop blaming other people for the disasters in his life and pay the price for his own sins of omission. For him, that meant taking the unselfish route now and walking away from yet another potential victim of his clumsy affections.

"There are some things," he said wretchedly, "that can't be fixed, my darling Pollyanna. Don't waste your love on a guy with a history of running out on his commitments when the going gets tough. I've forfeited the right to influence the terms by which other people choose to live their lives."

She drew in a great, ragged sob. "Self-pity is so unattractive," she said, searing him with her contempt. "So why don't you just forget it and call a spade a spade? You might fool yourself and a lot of other people into believing that warding off boa constrictors, pygmies and poisoned arrows makes you some sort of hero, but the plain fact is you're afraid of the responsibilities that love brings, and that makes you nothing but an emotional coward with a king-size ego, as far as I'm concerned. It's a lot easier to walk away from the risk of failure than it is to stay and lay bets on success, isn't it? Well, there's the door, Hugh. Don't let me keep you!"

Yesterday, he'd listened to Jane itemize his many shortcomings in painstaking detail. He didn't need this, as well. "You're pushing your luck," he warned. "You've got my daughter, which is what you've been after from the very beginning. Don't expect me to hand you my head on a silver platter, too."

She turned away from him, and said in a weary, disillusioned voice, "It wasn't your head I was interested in, Hugh, it was your heart—until I found out it was empty. Your loss, my mistake."

Then she went back to her desk, pressed the intercom, and calmly instructed her secretary to show him out. Short of making a scene that would change nothing, he had no choice but to leave.

The next morning, Nina watched with Jane and Sophie while Hugh finished loading up his car. Today, he started the long journey back east, and within the week he'd be flying back to Colombia.

"Be good," he said to Jane, hugging her. "I'll expect all As on your report card when I see you in December."

She stood stiffly within his embrace. They'd made peace of a sort, the night before, but it was a delicate thing requiring careful handling. "Yes, Daddy."

"Will you write to me?"

She shrugged, her expression remote. "I expect so."

"Do I get a goodbye kiss?"

Dry eyed, she offered her cheek. Awkwardly, he bent and touched his lips to it. Over her head, his eyes searched for and found Nina. The face, with its spare, masculine beauty which had never failed to startle her, was haggard. He was hurting.

Last night, they, too, had talked. It had been a calm, rational discussion that started out dealing with practicalities. Without intent, though, the conversation had slipped from their separate rights and expectations regarding Jane and her welfare into a more personal vein.

"Summer's almost over," Hugh had said, staring out to the western horizon where pink and turquoise ribbons of cloud slashed the sky. "I didn't think, at the start of it all, that things would end up quite like this."

Start. End. It was those two familiar, ordinary words that forced Nina to confront something she'd steadfastly ignored from the day he'd walked into her life. The summer had been a treasure chest and she'd lived it from moment to moment, dipping into it without once acknowledging that, sooner or later, the source must run dry.

"No," she'd replied, "I didn't think it would end this way, either."

"I'd like to think that, despite our differences, we've become friends. That's more than a lot of people, especially those in our situation, can say."

Friends, yes, but lovers, too. She wanted it all!

He came to her now and reached for her hand. For an instant, she thought perhaps he might take her in his arms. Instead, he gave her fingers a tight squeeze. "Take care of each other," he said thickly.

She would not let him see her cry. "Of course." Her gaze roamed over his face, memorizing every inch of it, knowing she'd never be able to look at Jane and find traces of him. It was both a curse and a blessing. "Take care of yourself," she said around the ache in her throat.

"I will."

He turned to Sophie, who waited to one side. For the first time he smiled and slapped the hard, flat plane of his stomach with the palm of his hand. "I've got you to thank for all these extra pounds, Sophie. Another month, and none of my clothes would fit."

Weeping unashamedly, Sophie enfolded him in ample arms and kissed both his cheeks. "*A bientôt, mon cher monsieur.*"

His composure almost cracked. "*Au revoir.*"

Then the goodbyes were over and there was nothing left to say. He climbed into the car, slammed shut the door, and was gone down the road with the sun silhouetting his head like a halo. They watched until he turned the corner at the bottom of the hill and disappeared from view.

"He didn't even stay for my birthday," Jane whispered, and turned to Nina with the tears streaming down her face. "It was easy for him to leave me, Nina."

Nina ached for father and for daughter. Absence of shared genes notwithstanding, they'd both been cast from the same stubborn mold. "No, darling," she murmured, her own tears pressing hot behind her eyes. "It was the hardest thing he's ever done."

"I don't see how," Jane sobbed. "He's done it so often before."

She was too young to see the loneliness in him, and too full of her own hurt to recognize his. It took hours to console her, hours which, God help her, Nina was loath to see end because when they did she had nothing left behind which to hide from her own sorrow.

"Madame Nina." Sophie's voice found her where she sat out on the terrace after Jane at last fell asleep. "It is almost midnight. Is there nothing I can get for you? A little herbal tea, perhaps, or hot milk?"

"Nothing, Sophie, thank you. Go to bed. It's been a long day."

"It has been a sad day," Sophie said, "and there will be, alas, more to come before the world is put right again."

It would never be right again, Nina thought, looking out across the pool to the dark windows of the garage apartment. Just when she thought she was over him, he'd come to mind, in the silence of long, dreary November nights, in the cheerful birdsong of summer dawns. Nothing would ever be the same again.

She'd miss his slow smile and the way it pooled warmth and humor into his eyes. She'd miss his arrogant certainty, his unexpected humility that never once failed to dilute her anger, his sensitivity and compassion. He was her shadow man, the counterpart that made her a whole woman. Without him, she would never be complete. There would always be an empty space in her heart that not even Jane could fill.

And in her arms, his lithe, elegant body next to hers? She shuddered at the thought of a lifetime of empty dreams from which she'd awake to find herself alone. The grief speared through her, and lowering her head into her hands, she cried as she never remembered crying before. He'd gone, and he'd taken all the bright, beautiful promise that was tomorrow with him.

*     *     *

Nothing overt alerted her to the knowledge of his return. Not the noise of his footsteps, because her ears were filled with the sound of her own weeping. Not his shadow that slanted long and narrow over the stucco wall of the garage, because when she lifted her head the moonlight dazzled her tear-filled eyes and blinded her.

It was her heart, the only true barometer by which to measure love, that told her he had slain his private dragons and thereby saved her having to grapple with hers. She knew, as surely as the sun would rise tomorrow, that he had come to terms with the fact that his destiny was interwoven with hers. Not because of their common bond with Jane, but because God in His wisdom had created them solely for each other independently of any other reason.

She rose to her feet, moving slowly at first like a sleepwalker. She had no memory of her arms reaching out to hold him, nor of the dew-drenched grass caressing the soles of her feet as she crossed the lawn. Yet, all at once, her body crashed against his, knocking the breath out of her, and his mouth was skimming over hers as though, if he didn't fill himself with the taste of her, he would die.

"I cannot leave you," he muttered, his voice rough with anguish.

There were a hundred questions to ask, a thousand healing words to say. Later.

He slipped one arm beneath her legs, swung her up into his arms and turned back toward the garage apartment. He climbed the stairs and lowered her to the bed, all the time holding her so close to him that every limb found its mate, every heartbeat its echo.

One touch was all it took for the warm ache of wanting to rush over her, pearling her skin with anticipation. Yet there was no haste, no greed, just a slow and grateful rediscovery of paradise. They undressed each other almost incidentally, knowing that, at last, there was all the time in the world to stop and wonder over the texture and design, the contour and symmetry of each other. How incredible the complexity, how singularly unique the beauty of what they made for each other.

Desire overtook them stealthily, stroking through them until their hearts pulsed with the dark rhythm of its craving. They fitted together so perfectly that it was hard to believe they'd ever doubted the absolute rightness of their being together. He buried himself in her, and she wrapped herself around him so tightly that not even the most slender moonbeam could find a way between them.

He did not take her to ecstasy. She did not follow, nor he attempt to lead. They raced together side by side toward a fulfilment neither would ever find except with each other. When the passion exploded, it was exhilarating, death defying, and it was lovely.

After, he stretched out one arm and flicked on the bedside lamp. He wanted them to see each other clearly, wanted to look deep into her eyes and clear through to her soul when he spoke. There'd be no more reluctant secrets muttered in the dark.

He stroked back the hair from her face, drew his finger over the sweep of her eyebrow and down the tender curve of her cheek. "I love you, Nina," he said. "I will love you for the rest of my life."

That made her cry again. "Oh!" She muffled the sobs against his shoulder and wound her arms tightly around him.

"Don't do this," he growled into her hair. "You know I can't stand it."

She cried harder. It seemed that, today, the tears of her entire adult life had burst through the dam that had kept them in check for so long. Every time she thought she had them under control and opened her mouth to tell him so, they came pouring out again even though, on the inside, her blood sang an anthem of joy at his words.

"I'm very happy," she assured him on a waterlogged hiccup, "and I feel like a fool for reacting this way. Turn off the light, please! I must look a mess."

"Not only that," he said, smiling that sweet, slow smile that had ensnared her from the first, "but you're wetting the bed! How am I going to explain this to Sophie?"

"Hugh!" Her squeak of dismay melted into a giggle. She mopped her face with the edge of the sheet and took a steadying breath. "What a romantic thing to say!"

He nuzzled her ear. "Well, it's not what I'd have chosen to fit the moment, but I'm afraid to tell you again how I feel about you in case you drown both of us."

"Tell me," she demanded, threading her fingers through his hair and holding his head captive. "I can handle it. I'm in control again."

"I love you." His voice grazed her mouth and his eyes adored her. "I want to spend the rest of my life with you."

She had to ask. It simply wasn't in her nature to take it for granted. "Are you sure?"

"Yes."

"How do you know?"

He rolled over onto his back and tucked her snugly against him. Should he tell her that he'd had to pull off the road that afternoon, because his eyes were glazed with tears for the first time in more than thirty years? That he'd realized, as he put the safety of miles between them, that he could run to the ends of the earth and never escape her?

He'd walked beside a lazy river and found a spot where tall evergreens shaded the bank. He'd sat there for an hour, maybe more, and taken stock of himself. He hadn't liked what he'd discovered: a man who'd vented the anger and resentment of half a lifetime on the one woman he loved with a depth and passion he'd never believed himself capable of. The knowledge had made him feel ill.

He'd thought back to the day he first saw her and known he'd never forget it as long as he lived. Not because it was the day that Jane had finally come face-to-face with her natural mother but because, contrary to everything in which he believed, instinct had told him he'd finally met the right woman, the only woman for him.

But because he was a pigheaded fool, he'd tried to ignore the fact and thereby extended his misery. He'd systematically set out to destroy the tenderness, the trust, the promise—all those things that built a foundation of endurance to last long after the heady rush of desire had sated itself. And she had loved him despite that.

He'd told himself that it was as well that he'd left Jane with her and was taking himself back to the jungle, the tundra, the desert—anywhere, as long as he was too far away to hurt those he loved the most. He was a good engineer, one of the best, which made him luckier than most men. In the past, that had always made up for being a lousy husband and father.

This time, though, that line of reasoning hadn't worked. Her voice had haunted him. "You're afraid of the responsibilities that love brings..." And he'd finally faced up to the fact that the only person standing between him and the happiness he deserved was himself.

He tipped her face up to his. "I couldn't stand the pain," he said simply. "Leaving you was tearing me apart."

"What about Colombia and your professional obligations?"

"What about priorities and the rest of our lives?" He dropped a kiss on her mouth, then another. "There are other engineers, but you and I have waited long enough. I can delegate someone else to take over the South American project, but no one's deputizing for me where you and I are concerned."

She was doomed to play devil's advocate. "But your work is important to you."

"Yes, it is." He toyed with her throat, delineated the triangle of her collarbones with persuasive fingers. His mouth was issuing facts, but his eyes held promises that made her blood race. "Remember the partnership with the Vancouver firm that I mentioned? Their offer still stands." His hand stilled at her breast. "I'm ready to accept it, but..."

"But what?" She traced the curve of his smile and was caught unprepared by the desire that snaked through her when he trapped her fingertip between his teeth and nipped gently.

"I want a wife, too. I'm all through with half measures and settling for second best. I want it all, and I want it now."

"Oh, good!" She stretched against him luxuriously, glorying in the fire that burned hot and sultry in his gaze. "I was afraid I was going to have to be the one to propose."

"Good God!" His hands raced over her, leaving expectation trembling everywhere he touched. "Did I actually propose?"

"Yes," she sighed, "and I accept. There's no going back."

"You're right," he said, his voice frayed with urgency. "There's no stopping now. Turn out the light, my darling."

# CHAPTER TWELVE

"DADDY, you remembered!" Jane's delight outshone the sun the next morning when she appeared for breakfast and found Hugh there waiting for her. "You came back for my birthday, after all."

Laughing, he caught her as she catapulted across the room, narrowly missing a jug of maple syrup on the table. "Among other things, yes."

"What other things?" Suspicion flared as she intercepted the glance he exchanged with Nina. "Did something happen?"

"Nothing bad," Nina assured her, and wished belatedly that they'd spared a moment from their own happiness to consider how it might affect Jane's. It had never occurred to either of them that she'd receive their news with anything less than delight. Until now. "It's just that——"

"I had to come back," Hugh said, reaching one hand out to cover hers and snagging Jane in the crook of his other arm, "because I want to be with Nina."

Jane flung off his touch, her eyes stormy. "I might have known it wasn't because of me."

"Look, Janie, you know I love you, and you know Nina loves you."

"So?" She huddled on her chair, drawing into herself and shutting them both out. "Big deal."

"Doesn't that matter to you?"

A pause that stretched unbearably, worse than waiting for an unsympathetic jury to hand down a decision, then, "I guess."

179

"Then isn't it nice and convenient that Nina and I love each other, as well?"

Jane shifted on her chair and condescended to look at him. "Maybe. It depends."

Hugh chose his words with care. "I hadn't forgotten your birthday, Jane, and I'm glad you want me here to help you celebrate it because, to tell the truth, I wasn't sure I was all that important to you. So let's not spoil this special week. Just for once, let's be happy."

"You already are," Jane muttered. "You don't need me, either of you."

"You're wrong," Hugh said, "but I know where you're coming from. I had a hard time accepting that Nina might find me lovable for myself and not because I was an unavoidable extra she was stuck with in order to get to know you." He reached for her again, and when she didn't pull away from him, went on, "You're a part of our lives and the reason we ever met. We'd still be strangers if it weren't for you. But just because you're my daughter doesn't give you exclusive rights to my affections."

Jane chewed on that for a while. "All this exclusive rights stuff," she said at length, "that's just your fancy way of saying we don't own each other, right? It's not up to me to decide who you fall in love with."

"Exactly." Hugh sighed with what Nina feared was premature relief. "I knew you'd understand."

A savvy gleam lightened Jane's eyes. "Sure, Dad. Just like you understand that just because you're my father doesn't mean you get to choose my friends, right?"

"Good God, we're talking about Rolando again!" Hugh exclaimed. "Nina, will you please explain how, in the light of what you claim to be your undying love, you can sit there with that smirk on your face and let me put both feet in my mouth like this?"

Nina smiled sweetly. "Because it'll be such fun watching you try to get them out again. Jane, my darling, you're a child after my own heart. Have you ever considered making a career out of law?"

"Actually," Jane replied with a cheeky grin, "I think I'd make a good psychiatrist."

They didn't belabor their plans for the future. There was no longer a deadline requiring that things be rushed to a speedy conclusion, and it seemed more important to allow everyone time to adjust to changes that would touch all their lives.

That night, when Nina peeped in to say good-night to Jane, she found her holding the framed photograph of Hugh and Sandra.

"Oh!" Guiltily, Jane hid the frame under the sheet.

"Hey." Uninvited, Nina sat on the bed and cupped her daughter's soft cheek. "It's okay."

Jane turned away miserably. "I still think about her sometimes," she said. "Does that make you hate me?"

"No, sweetheart, it makes me love you more. I'd be very disturbed if you were able to forget the mother who raised you just because I'm part of your life now. Just remember that I'm not taking anything away from her so much as carrying on from where she left off."

"I guess so." Jane brought out the photo and set it back beside her bed. "Is it okay if I keep her picture here?"

"Absolutely. I know she'd be very proud of you and the way you're handling all this. You've grown into a lovely young woman and she has to take a lot of the credit."

"Yes," Jane decided modestly. "I guess you're right."

*   *   *

The week slid by. Hugh signed a partnership agreement with the firm that had been courting him ever since he first arrived in town. Nina and Hugh took Jane to the local high school where they met the principal and a couple of the teachers. Jane came away thrilled that she'd be sharing classes with boys. Hugh wore his anxious father look at the mere idea.

In between times, Nina planned Jane's birthday for the following Saturday.

"In the morning, I've made an appointment for her at the beauty parlor," she confided to Hugh on Wednesday evening as they shared a quiet moment alone. "You might not have noticed, but she's trying not to chew her nails these days, so I've booked a manicure for her, then a hairdo. You could take us out for lunch, after, if you like. Then, for the evening, a dinner party at Giorgio's in the Park. It's such a glamorous, romantic restaurant."

"Is that what a sixteen-year-old really wants, glamour and romance?"

"Hugh, turning sixteen is momentous for a girl! It's the difference between scrambled eggs and omelets, knee socks and silk stockings, pajama parties and dates."

"Yes, well..." he looked, Nina thought, rather like a man suffering a bout of indigestion "...that being so, I suppose it would be all right—since we'll be there to keep an eye on things and all—if we let her invite an escort."

Nina snuggled up against him. "What would be nice, my wonderful man, would be if you invited Rolando to turn up as a surprise guest."

"You're pushing your luck," he advised her, and put himself safely beyond reach at the other end of the sofa. "I will not let you appeal to the animal lust in me in order to weasel me out of my good sense. However, just for the record, I'd already thought of doing exactly as you suggest."

"You're such a sensible man," Nina purred. "No wonder I love you so much."

"What else are we doing for her?"

"Giving separate gifts."

"Why?" He inched back towards her, the light of love in his eye. "Aren't we trying to project the concept of us as a couple, or is the honeymoon over before it's even begun?"

Nina wondered if there'd ever come a time when her flesh didn't quicken at his slightest touch. "It's important, I think," she explained, keeping her mind firmly on the topic under discussion, "that this year we show her that she's special to us as individuals. I plan to take her shopping tomorrow for a new dress, and I've also got an antique gold locket that belonged to my godmother that I'd like Jane to have. The only thing is, its chain got lost or broken years ago."

"Why do I get the feeling I'm being steered into the nearest jewelry shop to look for a glamorous, romantic chain?"

"Intuitive as well as sensible," Nina murmured, and slid into the curve of his arm to settle her head on his shoulder.

"Brilliant, too, my darling. It just so happens that a gold chain would go rather well with what I've already got for her."

"What's that?" She loved the clean smell of his skin, the crisp vitality of his hair.

"Earrings," he said. "Gold, of course. For pierced ears."

"Why do I find planning all this so much fun? Is it because I'm sharing it all with you?"

He dropped kisses on the crown of her head. "It occurs to me," he remarked, "that you're trying to make up in one day for the fifteen birthdays you missed—and perhaps to erase some rather unhappy memories of yourself at Jane's age. I can add up, Nina. You were just two months shy of your own sixteenth birthday when she was born."

He was the most perceptive man in the world, as well as the most handsome. She fell in love with him all over again.

She and Jane found the perfect dress, demurely alluring with a full, swirling skirt and fabric so finely woven that it stopped just short of sheer. The color, sea foam shot through with tropical turquoise, was marvelous with Jane's light tan and hazel eyes.

"I absolutely love it," she declared, pirouetting in front of the boutique's full-length mirror with unabashed admiration for the figure she cut.

Nina didn't need another outfit; her closet was already full. It was nothing but vanity and lack of will-power that prompted her to try on the little black dress with the spaghetti straps, and once it slithered over her body she was lost. It showed off her slender shoulders and gave her a waist that Twiggy would have killed for.

"Wow!" Jane rolled knowing eyes. "Wear that, and you'll knock Daddy's socks off!"

Saturday was one of those special days that came at the end of summer. Bees hovered drunkenly among the flower beds, the roses wore the jaded air of ageing debutantes, and it seemed impossible that within two months the trees would be stripped bare and the winter gales rolling in across the Strait. The sky had lost the hard-edged clarity of July and had a hazy softness to it that reminded Nina of Hugh's eyes after he'd made love to her.

Jane was thrilled with her gifts and wore them immediately, uncaring that antique lockets and walking shorts made for an odd combination. "Mother always said that gold is never out of place or fashion," she quoted, and didn't see the frown that passed over Hugh's face so quickly that it barely had time to register.

"How long will it take before you and I are elevated to Sandra's plane?" he grumbled, *sotto voce*, to Nina.

"I don't know," she told him, "nor am I about to ask. Be patient, my darling. It's early days yet and in any case, this is not a competition."

"I'm not cut out for patience. I want to put a ring on your finger and tell the whole world that you're mine without being made to feel as if I'm dancing on Sandra's grave."

In fact, he'd bought a ring just that morning, and it was burning a hole in his pocket. The only thing that prevented him from hauling it out and showing it off was the fear that it might provoke one of those reactions in Jane that so effectively soured her mood and spoiled the day for everyone else. He loved his daughter but he did not understand teenage girls, and he both envied and admired Nina's tolerance.

"Once the summer's over and Jane's settled down at school," he promised his soap-lathered face in the mirror later, as he shaved in preparation for the evening ahead, "it's going to be Mr. and Mrs. Hugh Cavendish. No more delays, and no more pussyfooting around."

When he saw Jane, though, his resentment, such as it was, vanished and he thought he was going to make a damn fool of himself. He hardly recognized the young woman who opened the front door to him when he drove around to pick up his passengers.

"Well," he said, clearing his throat and blinking like an owl, "don't you look like a princess! Will the back seat be acceptable for Her Royal Highness?"

"Perfectly, thank you," Jane replied with more composure than he'd been capable of when he was twice her age, and stepped daintily into the car, antique locket swinging from its new chain and gold earrings glinting.

Then Nina appeared, and the sight of her took his breath away. He'd seen her naked and thought nothing could stun him more, but he'd been wrong. The dress flowed over her like rich, dark chocolate encasing cream. It made his mouth water.

She wore crystals in her ears and at her throat, and a slim gold bangle on her wrist. The only thing missing, to his eye, was the emerald-cut diamond hidden under his socks in the dresser drawer of his bedroom.

"Don't prolong the evening," he threatened, stooping to kiss the side of her neck as he held open the car door for her, "or I'm likely to undress you right at the table. You are the most delectable woman I have ever seen."

Rolando knew how to make an entrance. They were barely seated, and were still admiring the flower arrangements scattered throughout the restaurant, when he arrived at their table. He wore his hair as usual, tied back in a sleek ponytail, but otherwise was scarcely recognizable in the dark suit and frosty white shirt that bore the determined stamp of Maria Torres's flat iron.

"Happy birthday, Jane," he said, except that he pronounced her name "Juana" in the Spanish style, and presented her with an orchid corsage.

Jane very nearly squealed out loud with delight when she discovered a filigreed silver butterfly nestling among the petals. Remembering herself just in time, she stammered out her thanks before diving behind the outsize menu until she'd composed herself. Then, she peeked out, pink cheeked and wide eyed. "Did you know Rolando was going to be here, Daddy?" she whispered anxiously.

"Of course." Hugh indicated the vacant chair next to Jane's. "Have a seat, Rolando. You're just in time."

*"Gracias, señor."* Rolando inclined his head at Nina. *"Señora*, you look magnificent, and Jane is unmistakably your daughter. I am honored to be included in your celebrations."

Nina smiled. "We're delighted you could join us, aren't we, Hugh?"

"Of course," Hugh repeated blandly, looking the picture of unlikely innocence.

After an excellent dinner, the waiter wheeled in the special birthday cake Nina had ordered, its sparklers shooting stars all over the trolley.

"This is absolutely the best birthday ever," Jane declared, flushed with an excitement that seemed to depend on something other than the knowledge that she was the centre of attention of just about every other guest in the place. "I love everything, all my gifts and the surprises, everything."

"We're glad," Hugh said. "We think you're rather special."

She squirmed, forgetting for the moment that she liked to think of herself as almost a woman. "But what makes it really special," she said, eyes dancing with a secret that wouldn't be contained a second longer, "is that my locket opens. Here, take a look, Nina."

She slipped the chain from around her neck and passed the locket to Hugh, who handed it over to Nina. "What's so special about that?" he asked, mystified.

"Nina knows." Jane's eyes remained fixed on Nina. "Don't you?"

Nina was quite unprepared for what she discovered. Despite all the thought she'd given to making this day special, it was Jane who gave the best gift of all. Two pared-down headshots from pictures taken over the summer filled the oval frames in each half. One was of Nina, the other of Hugh.

Embarrassing tears sprang to her eyes and she fumbled for her serviette. "Oh, Jane!"

"I was just trying to say that I love both of you and I think it's okay that you two want to be together," Jane exclaimed in horror. "I didn't mean to make you cry, Nina!"

"I'm not crying," Nina sniffed.

"She's crying," Hugh said with droll resignation. "It happens every time she hears those three little words. I don't know what I'm going to do with her."

"Whew!" Jane swiped a relieved hand across her forehead that left her fringe in total disarray. "Why don't you marry her, Dad, then you wouldn't have to say them so often?"

"I think that's an excellent idea," he said, "at least for the most part." He picked up his own serviette and dabbed at Nina's eyes. "What do you say, my darling Pollyanna? Are you still willing to take a chance on us?"

"Only if you promise not to stop telling me you love me."

"Damn," he said. "What's the use of a ring if it's hidden under a man's socks instead of on his lady's finger?"

"What?" Nina stifled a giggle.

"Never mind." He beckoned to the head waiter. "I just got engaged," he said, with magnificent disregard for the interested observation of diners at other tables. "I think that calls for a bottle of your very best champagne."

"I think so, too, sir." The man beamed and snapped his fingers for the wine steward. "On the house, of course."

While the wine was being poured, Hugh fashioned a ring from the gold foil torn from the neck of the bottle. He slipped it on Nina's finger, then turned over her hand and kissed her palm. "Thank you," he said, "for falling in love with me, for agreeing to be my wife, and for teaching me that it's never too late to be happy. You have given me back my daughter and a reason to look forward to the rest of my life."

"Oh, Hugh!" she whispered, eyes swimming.

Three serviettes changed hands around the table.

Relive the romance...
Harlequin® is proud to bring you

A new collection of three complete novels every
month. By the most requested authors, featuring
the most requested themes.

Available in October:

# DREAMSCAPE

They're falling under a spell!
But is it love—or magic?

Three complete novels in one special collection:

**GHOST OF A CHANCE by Jayne Ann Krentz
BEWITCHING HOUR by Anne Stuart
REMEMBER ME by Bobby Hutchinson**

Available wherever Harlequin books are sold.

HARLEQUIN PRESENTS®

*A Year*
DOWN UNDER

In 1993, Harlequin Presents celebrates the land down under. In October, let us take you to rural New Zealand in **WINTER OF DREAMS** by Susan Napier, Harlequin Presents #1595.

Olivia Marlow never wants to see Jordan Pendragon again—their first meeting had been a humiliating experience. The sexy New Zealander had rejected her then, but now he seems determined to pursue her. Olivia knows she must tread carefully—she has something to hide. But then, it's equally obvious that Jordan has his own secret....

Share the adventure—and the romance—of A Year Down Under!

Available this month in
**A YEAR DOWN UNDER**

**AND THEN CAME MORNING**
by Daphne Clair
Harlequin Presents #1586
Available wherever Harlequin books are sold.

YDU-S